THE EMPTY COFFIN MYSTERY

Soviet Gulag, Rejection, and Exoneration

Shane Woods Series
Book Nine

Author: Dr. Tom Latham
Editor: Dave Carlson

DynoTech Publishing, Colorado Springs, CO USA

Edited and published by Dave Carlson at DynoTech Publishing, Colorado Springs, Colorado, USA.
(www.dynotech.com)

ISBN: 978-1-885708-59-5 (Paperback)

Library of Congress Control Number (LCCN):
2026914125

Print information is available on the last page.

First Printing: June 2026

Contents

INTRODUCTION

I love storytelling. In my books, I aim to bring readers joy, encourage reflection on faith, and share real emotions inspired by true experiences—enhanced fictionally. My goal is to show Christ as the only true Savior and illustrate how sincere faith leads to a vibrant Christian life.

I am committed to presenting Christ as the only true Savior, and to showing that following Him wholeheartedly defines authentic Christian living. I also reveal the devastating impact the liquor industry had on my family, hoping to illustrate the destruction it can cause. It is a legal drug that sent my mother to prison; caused my brother, Danny, to take his life at 49 years old; and was the reason my cousin killed himself.

Abandoned four times by my mother, I found refuge with my loving grandparents at Crabtree Creek farm. Their care shaped my life. I have no idea where I would be today if it weren't for the tender care of my grandfather, John Taylor, and his wonderful wife, Julia. Certainly, I wouldn't be where I am.

This book is written to inspire you to accept Christ as your Savior and commit fully to Him. My own journey began on May 6, 1964, when fellow sailor Richard Edwards invited me to Calvary Baptist Church in San Francisco, California. During my Navy service, Richard and I shared our faith with others during sea voyages.

I spent ten years in formal Bible study. Our family arrived in Brazil on October 1, 1976, where we started four churches. I now pastor the fourth church while coaching wrestling at a public school.

I've always tried to follow traditional writing rules, but I recently discovered and like the concept of "poetic license." While I'll follow most accepted grammatical rules, I understand that, many times, it's my choice what to do with commas and when to insert or remove the word 'that' from a sentence."

I like pictures and the way they amplify my words. That's why my books have images. Images on otherwise blank pages that are not directly related to the storyline represent true-life events or objects that inspired many of my stories.

Most images and illustrations in this book were generated or enhanced using artificial intelligence (AI) technology to enrich your experience as a reader.

Dr. Tom Latham
Missionary and Wrestling Coach in Brazil

Chapter 1
SIBERIA

SIBERIA, just the mention of the word brought chills to the Russian people. Who was sent there? The ones who wanted to be free, criminals, and anyone else who looked cross-eyed at the KGB or the communist government leaders. The government started sending criminals and political prisoners there in 1865, the same year the American Civil War ended.

Up to the present date, over 14 million souls have suffered in the frozen wasteland of that Arctic region. Between 1929 and 1953, 14 million souls were run through the camps called "Gulags." During the period

1941-1943, at least 516,841 people died in these camps because of a lack of food and supplies during WWII.

The coldest recorded temperature in history was in Oymyakon, at a dreadful -96°F. The Trans-Siberian Railway was responsible for transporting these unfortunate condemned souls. A threat to be sent there was taken very seriously, and many who had the misfortune of being shipped there never returned.

It was towards this dreaded, frozen land that Loretta was headed. She had been unable to convince the KGB agents that she was not a CIA spy. Rudolf the Red was sure she had something to do with the Americans turning back the Russian warships, which were carrying guided missiles to Cuba.

He was about to crash a heavy code machine upon her head when he was interrupted by another agent. This intruder said something to Rudolf that left him without any options. The optionless Rudolf wrote a message on a yellow, lined notepad and walked out the door. No one saw Rudolf again or heard anything about him. It was like he had vanished off the face of the earth. No one missed him. Actually, the other agents threw a party to celebrate his disappearance. It was something they had wanted to do for decades.

Loretta decided to use her real name now. Using aliases had only gotten her deeper into a pit she was now finding impossible to climb out of. Historically, lying had served her well, at least this is what she'd always believed.

She developed into a shameless, bold-faced liar during her last two years of high school. It was a way to pass difficult exams without studying. Getting out of any trouble was easy for her. All she needed to do was 'invent a story' (as some had convinced her to start calling it).

But Gloria, her best friend in high school, called it downright sinful, a disgrace, that was only going to dig a deeper hole for her to try and crawl out of. "Listen, Girl, you're going down a road that has a BRIDGE OUT AHEAD sign, but you're bound and determined just to keep going! The decisions you're making now are developing a character that later will cause you to suffer a lot and will also cause a lot of suffering for everyone around you. Are you listening to me, Girl?"

Although she was her best friend, Loretta didn't take any of her advice. She always thought that any ditch she found herself stuck in, she could get out of by manipulation and deception. Loretta had mastered these tools of the trade, finding them very helpful in keeping her head above water while everyone else was drowning in their problems.

Even half-truths would work sometimes. For instance, when her dad asked her if she did her homework, she'd always answer, "yes." She knew he was actually asking if she had FINISHED her homework. But since he didn't use those exact words, She could get out of trouble by saying 'yes' because she had started her homework, even if she hadn't finished it. This trick worked on the few who trusted her implicitly.

Her first instinct was always to respond to Gloria with a smart-aleck answer. "I'm listening, I'm listening, all right, already, enough! You need to come down off your soap box long enough to be my friend instead of my priest."

Gloria wasn't lacking in quick responses either, "I wish pants really did catch on fire. It would make it a lot easier for all the rest of us honest folks to recognize a 'liar, liar, pants on fire' situation."

Now she discovered that no amount of lying would get her off the rusty, broken-down cattle car that was taking her further and further from the direction she really wanted to go—toward Lacomb, Oregon, the farm where she was raised. That refuge seemed like light-years away.

She'd gladly be a maid in the house of her father, rather than be in this cattle car with these hungry, desperate souls on their way to the frozen Siberian wasteland.

When she was a teenager, she was assigned to do the cooking, laundry, and housework for her lumberjack father and her two brothers, Walter and Jackie. She started this indentured servitude at the young tender age of nine because her mother had been a runaway, never to return. It reminded her of the Disney story "Cinderella." But that fairy tale had a different ending from her real-life tragedy.

She didn't have a fairy godmother or a beautiful chariot to take her to the ball. She didn't even have a bicycle to take her to Snow Peak Bridge to fish and swim. Loretta had to walk three miles along the logging road, dodging the mammoth trucks loaded with huge Douglas fir trees.

Her brother, Walter, always told people, "We're so poor, our pancakes only have one side." This always got a few laughs from the insensitive knuckleheads, which made Loretta mad. It wasn't fun to work all summer picking strawberries, raspberries, blackcaps, plums, apples, cherries, bush beans, and pole beans to buy her low-class apparel at Polly Potter's Used Clothing Trailer.

All these thoughts occupied her mind as she rumbled on northward, the temperature getting colder as each mile took her further into the frozen Siberian wilderness. She'd heard horror stories of this place she was going to have to call home, for how long, only God knew.

She'd thought of God more recently. Especially considering how many times she'd been rescued from sure death. The first time it happened was at the hands of Vini the Fin, the mafia goon who wanted his $10,000 back. She hadn't been blessed with the same poker face as her opponents; therefore, she lost more than she won, thus, her insurmountable debt to Vini. She had to run for her life.

The second time was when a San Francisco trolley car busted a cable, and she went zooming to her death. It was the huge NEW brakeman who forced the trolley to smash into car after car, from side to side, to try and slow the runaway trolley down. After he succeeded in this nearly impossible task, he gave her a solemn warning. "Get your life right with God before you face your ultimate demise."

Another two times, she had been saved by a floating coffin in the ocean, which gave her refuge from freezing to death in just 20 minutes, as a maid, Natasha, had warned her she would if she fell into the North Pacific. But Loretta hadn't just fallen in; she was pushed. Natasha believed Loretta was cheating at poker, so she threw her worst adversary overboard.

The last time was just a few days ago when Rudolf the Red was determined to split her head open with the heavy code machine. All these rescues had something to do with divine intervention. She'd been convinced of this. Now she was absolutely positive that God existed and that He was looking after her. Apparently, she had a guardian angel who spoke both perfect English and Russian.

She knew God was real. This was a new experience for her. Now she had to figure out just exactly WHO He was and what He wanted from her, if He really wanted anything at all, she wasn't sure of that part yet.

Being in this cattle car wasn't a pleasant experience; it wouldn't have been even for cattle. The difference was that cattle had their own leather jackets with a thick heating system underneath, and she only had a thin windbreaker. Even though she had little to keep her warm, she had more than some of the shivering, miserable Russians who were in her car.

She had taken their cue and huddled up to keep warm. The men were at one end of the car, and the women were at the other end. The freezing wind whipped through the cracks in the walls and roof. It was absolutely unbearable at night. In the early morning, when the sun began to shine its welcoming rays, squeezing through the cracks, all of them would jostle for the most luminous spot.

During the colder nights, she thought her feet and hands were going to freeze and fall off. She couldn't even feel them anymore. The Trans-Siberian Railroad had several stops on its way to the Gulag. At every stop, each person was given one sweet potato, two slices of bread, and a bottle of water that looked like lemonade; it was so dirty.

The Russians in her car were very friendly, giving her all the warmth they could muster. She couldn't converse with any of them, but they all managed to communicate with hand motions, smiles, and winks. Why were these wonderful people headed for the same concentration camp as she was? She, at least, was accused of being a CIA spy. Of what could these beautiful people be guilty?

There was no way of knowing how long this unbearable, freezing trip would take. It had already been three days. They must have passed the Arctic Circle by now. Loretta had experienced some cold weather in Oregon, but this was the most brutal and unbearable climate she'd ever seen. It never entered into her rebellious head that she could ever be this cold. She wondered how long the trip would be.

She didn't have to wonder very long. At noon on the fourth day, the train stopped because it had run out of track. This was the end of the line; the end of the world as she had known it. Some men were working on the track to complete a roundabout for the train to turn around.

The Soviet soldiers, protected from the cold by their heavy parkas, fur-lined hats, and gloves, opened the sliding door and stepped onto the ramp. They began yelling and waving their rifles, expecting their fellow citizens to lumber off the train like a herd of cattle. This was disgusting and immoral, but what could she do? She joined the herd.

The soldiers used their rifles to separate the men from the women, motioning for all groups to run into the barracks that decorated the barren yard. There were guard towers on every corner, manned by two men who were filling their area with the vapor from their breathing. Loretta was sure they weren't as miserable as any of their fellow Russians being herded into the dark, dingy living quarters.

It was lunchtime when they arrived. After they deposited their meager belongings on a flimsy bunk, they were pushed outside again for roll call. Standing in the dirt, shivering, they each had to call out their name loud enough for the hard-of-hearing commandant to mark them present. What were they worried about? Did these brain-dead masters think that one of their prisoners would actually escape, across a thousand miles of frozen wilderness?

She decided to use her real name. She wasn't ashamed of it. She bellowed out so all could hear, "Loretta Woods, American," just in case they didn't know.

The food in the dining hall was better than the miserable fare they had been given on the trip. At least this included hot, dirty water they called "coffee."

After lunch, they were given some warmer clothing. At first, she thought they might have started being nice, but afterward, she'd find out that the heavier clothing was meant to keep them alive so they could work in the salt mines.

The evening was spent huddling around the potbellied stoves. Some had saved a few veggies from previous meals, so they could put them in a pot and have a snack

before bedtime. Loretta was pressed up against a heavy-set woman whose face was partly hidden by a checkered scarf. The portly Russian jabbed her in the ribs and motioned for Loretta to follow her.

> ***AUTHOR NOTE:*** *The actual conversation from the Russian prisoner is in broken English. But, to make it easier for you to follow the story, I have printed it in clear, unbroken English.*

When they had gotten to the far corner of the barracks, the lady removed her scarf, revealing the left side of her face, which had horrible scars from her chin to her forehead. "You're an American, right? Please tell me that you're an American. I love Americans." The lady gave her a crooked smile, the best she could do with all the scars she was saddled with.

Loretta began to tear up. Her heart started beating a little faster, too. "Wow, someone who can speak English. Wonderful!" She was loaded with questions. "What's your name? Do you have any family? Why are you here? How long have you been here?"

"Whoa, there now, Missy. I can only answer one of your questions at a time. My name is Natalia. I'm here because my husband was a pastor and the government hates religious people. I've been here for five years, and my husband and children are all gone. They all perished in the camps. I'm the only survivor."

The American couldn't hold it back; she began to cry softly so no one else could hear her. The Russian lady put her hand on Loretta's shaking shoulder and looked directly into her misty eyes. "And you, what's a nice American lady like you doing in a horrible place liked this?" She was baffled to say the least. "Are you a Christian? Many Americans are Christians, aren't they?"

Loretta sniffed and tried to get her composure back, "The KGB thinks I'm a CIA spy. I'm not, but there's no way of proving that to them. To answer your last question, I believe in God, that makes me a Christian, doesn't it?" She was hoping the pastor's wife would answer in the affirmative.

Natalia was very careful about how she answered the American. She didn't want to make her mad or disappoint her in any way, "Missy, I am not a pastor, but if you want, we can study the Bible together. That is one of the things I have been able to hide from the guards. Would you be interested in studying God's Word with me?"

Loretta put her arm around her newfound friend. What a wonderful person God had put in her path. This would be a new experience, studying the Bible. And what an experience it would be, too. Imagine trying to explain to her family that she was studying God's Word with a Russian pastor's wife in a communist concentration camp in the middle of the frozen Siberian tundra. No one even knew she was here.

That night, she lay down on matted bedding with a horse-hair blanket that almost covered her. To keep her feet warm, she had to pull her knees to her chest, hoping her nighttime movements wouldn't reveal any part of her body. She hoped the mattress wasn't loaded with bed bugs and fleas. How could they survive this cold?

Before the sun began to peek over the wooded, frozen horizon, the lady guard started banging on the cold potbellied stove with her club. “Get up, you lazy women. Get up and get out of here so you can eat some oatmeal and get down to the salt mines.”

Loretta couldn't understand any of the cruel matron's orders. She'd have to follow Natalia's lead, trusting that the pastor's wife would keep her out of trouble. This female guard looked about as friendly as Rudolf was, and he was a beast, to be sure. With this idea in mind, the only American prisoner in this facility headed for the dining hall.

After gulping down their gruel, the women were led away to clean the ice off all the sidewalks in the Gulag.

The weather had gotten worse since they had arrived. It was -53° at night and warmed to a balmy -25° in the afternoon heat.

Even in the best of times, it was still bone-chilling cold in the late afternoon. Working from sunup to sundown had not been a practice that Loretta had ever wanted to become accustomed to, and certainly not here in the tundra of the most feared place in the entire world. She hoped the weatherman would be kinder to them than he had been recently.

With little time to themselves, the ladies would spend it in gossip, smoking, or reliving past luxuries. Natalia had another strategy in mind. She was going to study the Bible with her American friend, Loretta. This should be very interesting.

They hovered in the corner, under a 22-watt bulb, just enough light to read the Bible. The teacher began, “Do you believe the Bible is the Word of God? It is important that you believe this so we can get the most out of our study time.” She hoped that her poor English wouldn’t hinder this American’s understanding of what the Bible said about itself.

Loretta just shook her head. “I have no experience with the Bible. I’ve never studied it and have never even considered it to be a book that God wrote. Did He write it, really? Did He?”

“Well, He didn’t write it Himself but He did use the Holy Spirit to move in the hearts of men so they wrote what He wanted them to. You’ll have to trust me to translate some verses for you. Can you trust me, Loretta?”

Loretta had no choice, but also didn’t doubt that this humble, wonderful woman would translate accurately what was written in the Russian Bible: “So, tell me how you know absolutely, without a shadow of a doubt that God wrote this book and only this book.”

The teacher continued, “There are many religious books in the world, each one says that God wrote it. What’s the proof that the Bible is the only one God wrote? I’ll tell you what the proof is, and you’ll not be able to refute it, not in a hundred years.”

Just then, the lights went out. This meant they had

one minute to get into their bunks and button their lips. The matron would be by in just a few minutes to punish anyone who was a slacker in obeying this order.

It was difficult to tell when the building lights were off because the bright security lights outside the windows never went out. Even though it never got very dark inside the building at night, they worked so hard during the day that sleep came easily, even on empty bellies.

Loretta just made it under the horsehair blanket when the communist guard began making a drum out of their potbellied stove. She'd have to wait for the next lesson to get her answer.

Over the next two days, the ladies had to work in the salt mines below the surface. It was actually warmer down there than in the path of the wind topside. Above ground, there was a constant, irritating wind blowing off the flatlands. This made their hats fly off during roll call. Loretta used an old shoelace to keep her hat on her head.

The second lesson was going to have to produce the answer she was looking for. What is the proof, the indisputable, undeniable proof that the Bible is the Word of God, that it is His message to us, telling us what He wants us to know about Him.

Natalia had a lot to say about this subject. Having been a pastor's wife for 30 years, she had dealt with many people with the same questions as this American. She whispered lowly, "The greatest proof that the Bible is the Word of God is PROPHECY. The Bible has 4,000 prophecies, and 1,500 are still in the future."

Now she was giving Loretta new information, information she'd never even considered before. "What prophecies are you talking about?" Now the Russian had her attention. Would she be able to retain it?

"For instance, the birthplace of Christ, the fact that He died between two bad people and the fact that He rose from the dead three days after he was killed. These are all prophecies that cannot be disputed." She wondered if this was getting through to Loretta or was it running off her like water off a duck's back.

Loretta had never heard this before; this idea had never even entered her thinking, mainly because she didn't go to church, and the Bible wasn't a book she had spent any time reading. Why would she anyway? It never interested her one bit. Now she was captivated by this new information. Was the Bible really God's message to us? She was beginning to see through the fog now.

Natalia kept sharing more information. "No other religious book has even ONE prophecy, NOT ONE. The

Apostle Peter said in his second book, chapter one verse twenty-one, 'For the prophecy came not in old times by the will of man; but holy men of God spoke as they were moved by the Holy Spirit,' does this answer your questions, Loretta?"

They were both so intensely occupied with their Bible study that they didn't see the communist matron slip up behind them. She ripped the Bible out of Natalia's hand and tore it in two, right at the seam,

"This is what we do with this book of fables and lies. And as for you two, it will be three days working with no food." She was serious, and Natalia made sure Loretta knew that when she translated the guard's threats.

Before Loretta was ushered to her bed, she was able to whisper in Natalia's ear, "Good lesson, teacher. I believe the Bible is the Word of God." With that message ringing in her mind, the pastor's wife gave the American a smile and a double thumbs-up gesture.

Chapter 2
Hiding in Boise

"Being called a religious fanatic isn't the worst thing that can happen to a Christian, Billy," Shane was explaining to the spindle-legged, pint-sized wrestler. "What's worse is if you were tried for being a Christian and there wasn't enough evidence to convict you."

Billy looked at his best friend, but couldn't see him. He'd been born blind. In fact, his blindness was the chief reason he had been so bitter against God. He never understood how God could be the loving person all these kids said He was if He allowed him to be born blind. It just didn't calculate in his analogical brain.

While they were stranded on a ledge in Montana, he was finally persuaded to accept the existence of God. It was then, at that very instant, the thick, ever-present cloud cover cleared, and they were rescued. Billy was blind but not dumb in any stretch of the word. He thought his IQ was at least 140. He had a friend who worked in the school office take a peek at his records. Therefore, he could "see" the handwriting on the wall, or in this present case, in the snow.

Shortly after that, he heard a Jewish missionary explain the plan of salvation, and he accepted Christ as the promised Messiah. Billy didn't just receive Christ. After the very moment he was saved, he blurted out, "This is great, I'm going to give Christ my whole life." No one doubted he was saved, and no one questioned his statement concerning Christ. Why would they?

He had not shut up about it since that day. He was bold in his witnessing. He had given out Bible tracts to several people along the route and even asked whether they were interested in spiritual things. This took a lot of courage, especially since he had only been saved for a few days. Usually, new Christians took years to build up such spiritual courage.

But, on the other hand, he was very preoccupied about facing his Jewish parents. They weren't just hiding the fact that they were Jews, they also hated anything to do with religion, let alone religious fanatics like these Lacomb kids. His parents always called them names; he just ignored their comments, knowing any defense on their behalf would've started a debate he wasn't willing to engage in, one he felt he could never win.

He kept reminding them, "You just can't imagine the terrible fight that's going to occur when I tell my parents I've accepted Jesus Christ as the promised Messiah. It'll make Custer's Last Stand look like a picnic on the prairie."

Lieutenant Colonel George Custer and his troops were defeated by the Lakota Sioux and Northern Cheyenne tribes at the Little Bighorn, South Dakota, on June 25, 1896.

Erin tested Billy. “Maybe you shouldn’t tell them; you know, be a secret disciple.” Everyone else gave Erin an incredulous look, but she just waved them off, signaling for them to keep their cool, relax, take it easy. I know what I am doing.

“All right, Erin,” Billy caught her off guard, “do you think for one minute I’m taking you seriously. You’re just testing my dedication to Christ. No, there won’t be any mediocrity in the Christian life of Billy Evans.

“If you guys have taught me anything, you’ve taught me that being ho-hum for Christ isn’t acceptable. If I’m going to be a part of this club, this Christian do-gooder’s club, I need to be as on fire for Christ as all of you are. I’m sure Jesus would be very sad if I was afraid to claim Him as my Messiah. I read somewhere in the New Testament where He said, 'If you deny me, I'll also deny you before my father, which is in heaven,' or something similar to that. I'm not sure exactly what that means, but I'm not willing to find out.

"After all He's done for me, how can I be so small not to give Him my all?" Now, Billy was sounding like a hymn writer. He was also talking like the rest of them. That was fine and dandy now, but he knew there'd be a high price to pay for this attitude of giving his whole life to Christ, no holds barred and no turning back.

"You're too smart for me, Billy," Erin complimented the new convert. "Do you really think it'll be that serious with your parents? Does accepting Christ automatically mean the whole town needs to know your family is Jewish? I'd think that one fact wouldn't have anything to do with the other."

"Do you know what happened on August 6, 1945?" They all shook their heads in the negative direction. Billy got good grades in history. He always said history couldn't be changed, but other subjects like science and physics were always being updated, to the chagrin of their dedicated followers.

"For your information, that's when the United States Air Force dropped an atomic bomb on Hiroshima, a

Japanese city. Well, that's what's going to happen at my house when my atheist parents find out I now believe in Jesus. You ain't seen nothing yet.

"The last thing they warned me about before our trip was letting you guys influence me; make a religious fanatic out of me. I do believe it was God Himself who was influencing me. You guys didn't have anything to do with all the circumstances. You just invited me along. God took care of the rest. But it's not going to be easy to convince them when they don't even believe in God.

"Do you get the drift of my reasoning? If not, I'll keep on explaining it until you do. You need to realize what I'm going to have to go up against—a brick wall of atheism and hatred of anything that smacks of religion, not just yours, ANY religion."

Bowie didn't see why Billy was so concerned. "I was raised with many Nez Perce traditions. There was a lot of Spiritism involved in our family history. When I accepted Christ, my parents weren't upset. In fact, they've really encouraged me to be dedicated to my 'religion,' as they call it. Aren't you a little bit too worried about this, Billy?"

"You guys don't know my Dad. Ever since we moved from New York, he's worked hard to conceal the fact that we're Jewish. He even changed our name from Evanstein to Evans. He thinks that if people knew we were Jewish, it'd ruin his business. If you think for one minute he's going to ignore my decision for Christ, then you REALLY don't know my Dad.

"Not only does he want to continue to hide the fact that we are Jewish, but he also despises the world's religions. He claims that Hitler was a Protestant, and look what he did to our people. No, Siree Bob, he's not going to be a bit pleased to know what I've done. It'll be a miracle if I even get to stay at home."

The kids were very concerned because they had finally accepted that Billy knew exactly what he was talking about. They became absolutely convinced when they saw him start to perspire and tremble a little as he described his Dad. But being thrown out of house and home seemed a bit of an overstatement. Not one of them could even fathom this happening to an only child.

Kosy, always the most tenderhearted, tried to pledge her support. "Listen, Billy, it may be rough, but we're with you all the way. We won't just pray for you, we'll also do anything we can to support you in any way possible. Right gang?"

Everyone gave a hearty "amen" to Kosy's promise of moral and spiritual support for the new Christian. No one but Billy really knew how horribly angry his Dad could get when it touched on religion. He had been an avowed atheist since the holocaust.

There was NO way Solomon Evans was going to accept this decision as Bowie's parents did. He was a determined, unwavering, hard-nosed atheist, and there wasn't anyone on Earth who could change his mind. Actually, no person on Earth changed Billy's mind either. Even the half-pint grappler admitted it. God had set up the circumstances that led him to reject evolution, believe in creation, and accept the Creator's Son, Jesus Christ, as his only and sufficient Savior.

The next day, there'd be an early-morning flight to Boise, Idaho, and then over the Cascade Mountains to Eugene to meet some very thankful parents and grandparents. The kids' rescue, including all the details, was statewide news in Oregon, Idaho, and Montana.

The Oregonian, the state's most important paper, had published several articles on the kids' disappearance and rescue. These well-read stories are what really ticked off Engelbert Farnsworth III. He spouted off to his brainless companions, "They're at it again, making themselves famous, all over the state. These so-called Christians make me sick to my stomach. I'll have to plan more fun and games for them. If any of you have an idea of what we can do to make their lives miserable, let me know." No one did at that very moment, but they all promised to work hard on the project!

There had been several opportunities for the survivors to give their testimonies. For his own sake, the kids kept Billy in the background. They didn't want his parents to find out about his spiritual decision on the TV or the radio. All six of them thought it'd be better for him to tell them personally, which he planned to do.

Ken Tanner, Edna Lynch's brother, didn't like the fact that the kids had missed most of their vacation. "All six of you'll have to come back here someday and really make up for the time you spent on the ledge. I know that time was well spent, but I had many other plans for you."

"Maybe we'll come back in the summer," Shane offered with a smile. "That way, if I fall in the creek, I'll just stay there." He got a lot of crooked smiles looking directly at him, and he deserved it.

The commercial flight out of Bozeman left as scheduled. This was going to be a good time. They were comparing the two experiences when the flight attendant stopped to talk to them. "Aren't you the six kids who were stranded in the ravine last week? I followed the whole ordeal and found it very fascinating. Finding you guys certainly was a modern-day miracle, to say the least."

Billy was sitting in the aisle seat. "Yes, that's right, lady. We're the famous survivors of the crashed 401 Cessna." We give all the credit to God for our miraculous rescue. Would you do yourself a favor and read this tract? It would mean a lot to us if you did." She gladly took the THIS WAS YOUR LIFE tract.

The others were smiling and shaking their heads in utter astonishment. Billy had really made a quick 180-degree turn. He'd become an outspoken "religious fanatic," as some would definitely call him. If he kept this up, he might even pass all of them. That was fine as far as they were concerned.

There was no jealousy on their parts. Anyone who wanted to be more evangelistic than they were used to being was welcomed with open arms to start a new fad among them. Anyone who wanted to be more spiritual than they have been would be an example to them.

The flight attendant was so impressed she felt she had to do something. "Listen, you kids, your story is so amazing, and your willingness to give God the glory is absolutely fantastic. This is so unusual to see in teenagers. I'm going to upgrade all of you to first class. Get your belongings and follow me." They didn't need anyone else to confirm her invitation. They all hauled their thankful bodies to the front of the plane and settled down for a great first-class return trip.

The mid-winter flight over the Rocky Mountains and Custer National Forest was breathtaking. The recent December snow, the same tonnage that had buried the Cessna from view, lay like a brilliant white quilt that had a few lumps in it. They were one of these lumps when they were stranded on the ledge.

When they started to land, Marty leaned over to Bowie. "I wonder if this pilot could fly through a ravine with only one hundred feet to spare on each side, land on a ledge, and not have any casualties?"

"He could if God had His hands on the yoke," Bowie was willing to give the credit where it was due. Marty was beginning to admire this big kid's attitude. He felt Bowie would be a great Christian someday; he already had a very good start. Even though he was the only Christian in his family, he was a good example of a young follower of the Nazarene.

Bowie disappointed all his Spiritist relatives when he refused to undergo the ritual of choosing his spirit name. It was a simple matter of following Christ or seeking help from the dark side, the side contrary to Christianity, against all that the Bible clearly teaches.

Although he was a new believer, the battle lines were drawn, and the decision was solid. “I’ll follow Christ, I’ll not meddle with the spirit world. This is MY decision, and I WILL stick to it. End of discussion as far as I’m concerned.” Nobody really wanted a battle with the huge rodeo champion.

Although Ana Pinetree, his cousin, was not a Christian, she defended Bowie’s right to decide his own destiny. She didn’t take his side just because she admired his courage, but also because when she wanted to make future decisions on her own, which might be questioned, she expected the same support from him and the same freedom from her relatives that he had received.

There’d be a three-hour layover at the Boise airport. The kids had only one thing on their mind—find out as much as they could about Ron Thomas, if that was possible. They left Billy at the cafeteria to do the questioning there. The rest split up to cover the whole airport to ask about the mysterious worker who had now disappeared.

Shane went to the personnel department. “I’d like to find out where the man who worked in the cafeteria lives. I think he’s an old neighbor of ours from Berlin, Oregon. His name is Ron Thomas. He’s the one with the long scar on his right hand, between his thumb and index finger.”

The secretary thumbed through her records. “We don’t have anyone here by that name. We don’t list our employees by their scars, so that information isn’t very helpful. Oh, here it is, under the name Thomas Jahn. You must've gotten it backward."

Shane excused himself for being so uninformed. He didn't want to say too much. "Could you give me his home address and telephone number, please?" This was his shot in the dark. He knew this information would be hard to get.

"We aren't allowed to give out that information about our employees. But wait a second, he quit just last week. That's funny, he only worked here for seven days. I suppose I could give you the name and address of an ex-employee, now, couldn't I?"

Shane thought, "Not really, lady, but I'm not going to stop you." Shane wasn't going to argue with her either. He took the information, thanked her for being so helpful, and met the others at the Northwest Orient ticket counter. They all had some information about the elusive neighbor.

He was known as Jonathan Thomas at the ticket counter, where he had purchased a ticket to Portland just last week. Around the baggage terminal, where he also put in some hours of overtime, he was known as Timothy Thomas.

Billy got the most information. "He worked here for only seven days. He was quiet, so no one ever learned anything about him. He claimed to be a drifter who was trying to settle down. Why would a man who ripped off an insurance company have to work in a place like this for minimum wage?"

"We don't know how much the settlement was," Erin commented, "or do we, Shane? Those details could be easily found by looking in the *Lebanon Express*. There's one thing we know for sure, though. Since there was a settlement, someone had to be involved to collect it, right? Then that other person is just as guilty of fraud as Ron Thomas is."

Kosy scratched her head. "That still doesn't answer the question of why a person who gets a lot of money from an insurance company would work at such a low-paying job as this. Why these people working here must not get more than $1.00 an hour."

Four more of them started scratching their heads and making fun of the new Charlie Chan in the group. "All right, you guys, I'll come up with some answers, and then you'll really be scratching your heads, wondering how I did it, okay?"

The rest of the trip was without incident, and that was just fine as far as six kids were concerned. The reunion at the airport in Eugene was full of hugs, kisses, and backslaps. Edna Lynch was crying, as was Grandma.

That's what made these women so special.

The last time they saw Billy, he was being escorted to his parents' new Cadillac. They had the dough all right. They had been successful in establishing several jewelry stores in Linn County. Evan's Jewelry was worn by almost all the residents of Lebanon and Albany. There'd be a tremendous inheritance for Billy someday. He answered the phone using a tape recorder to take orders, and gave out general information about the store's stock.

When the crew got to Rocking L Ranch, Edna showed the kids where she had buried Speedy, the hero pigeon. Kosy was all choked up when she prayed, "God, we thank You for this little pigeon. Without his courageous flight, we'd still be on a cold and lonely ledge in the dense Pioneer Mountains."

Then it was party time. Marty had even invited the Pinetree family to participate. It was the first time Travis and his whole family had been at the ranch. "Reminds me of my teen years on the ranch we had on the Nez Perce reservation in Northern Idaho.

"That's where I learned to track animals. I was taught by the greatest tracker of all of the Nez Perce. His name was Painted Pony, a relative of Chief Joseph. He was so good, he could track a bird in the sky." Travis knew that was an exaggeration; he was seeing if the group was paying attention.

Marty was not fooled, "Yeah, right. That would have made him the first air traffic controller, wouldn't it?"

Travis was glad someone was listening closely. "That is right, Marty. You're certainly awake today. I also began archery lessons there with his son, Running Buffalo. I was the one who got Bowie interested in shooting. But my son passed us all by, as far as hitting the bullseye. Bowie is really good."

Marty and Shane were going to make the best of the eats. In two days, they'd have to report to the scales in the high school locker room, ready to give an account of their vacation food vigil. They'd done fairly well when they were on the ledge, eating deer jerky and Oregon berries, but since then, they'd made up for lost time.

The scales wouldn't lie; they still had a lot of work to do. Now Bowie was another story. He needed to gain at least 20 pounds to be back in shape. Shane just sneered at the big Nez Perce. "Bowie, you make me sick—heavyweights!" Bowie didn't take offense at that remark; he just asked them to pass him two more pieces of pizza and a milkshake.

"Listen, little guy, pip-squeak, I'm on a strict diet to lose ten pounds this month. I only have fifteen to go," the heavyweight smiled. That made everyone smile, but it wasn't a knee slapper.

Mr. Lynch was taking pictures for the newspaper. “The reporter assigned to the story wants to interview all six of you kids. There’ll be at least a full page dedicated to your experience. It’ll be a wonderful opportunity to give your testimonies.” They all knew Billy would have to be left out of the interview for his own well-being.

When the Pinetree family left early, the kids rounded up the rest and gathered in the living room. Marty was the spokesman for the group. “We really have to pray for Billy. We couldn’t tell you everything over the phone, but he’s going to have a really rough time.

“His Dad has been hiding the fact that they are Jewish. According to Billy, Solomon Evans won’t like it even one little bit that his son has become a Christian. This is as serious as it could be, folks.”

Meanwhile, at the end of Rose Street, where all the rich people have their expensive homes, along the canal, Billy Evans was telling his parents all about the trip. “We were fortunate that Bowie was sitting in front instead of me. He even had a few lessons in flying before the pilot died.” This was only one of the many “coincidences” that had to happen to save all of their lives. He was trying to make his point before he put God in the equation, but doubted he was making any difference.

Mrs. Evans was glad to have her son back alive. “You can thank your lucky stars for all of that.”

Billy knew he’d have to tell them sometime, just how and when, he wasn’t sure. It was frightening to face his father. Solomon Evans, or Evanstein as it really was, wouldn’t be anyone to trifle with, especially when the subject was religion, any religion.

Billy said a silent prayer and plowed ahead. “We know that God answered our prayers; it was too miraculous to be a mere coincidence.” This would be the first small test.

Solomon Evans’ face flushed beet red. His appearance was contorted. He looked at poor Billy with fire in his eyes. “What did you say? I certainly hope I didn’t really hear what I think I heard.”

Billy started to stutter. He was hoping the kids had kept their promise to pray for him. “I ... I said we were definitely protected by the hand of God throughout our trip. It was no accident that all of those things were provided. God was watching over us.”

Solomon Evans angrily crashed his fist on the kitchen table. He was more violent than Billy had ever thought he could be. The situation was much more tense than Mrs. Evans could handle. She left the room in a hurry. Closing the door of her bedroom, she began pacing the floor. This was her way of handling stress; Billy had used the worry beads. Solomon had no stress outlet. He was the cause of most of the family stress.

"No son of mine is going to bring religion into this house." Billy knew he was about to be a victim of another atomic bomb blast just like he had described to the others. It was already bad, and he hadn't even mentioned that he had put his trust in the Messiah, Jesus Christ.

The next day, *The Oregonian* printed the article about the ravine rescue.

The Weather
Cloudy, occasional rain
High in the mid 40s
Low in the mid 30s
Details on Page 2.

The Oregonian

ESTABLISHED 1850

City Final
10 Cents
★★★★★

108th YEAR, NO. 2 — PORTLAND, OREGON, WEDNESDAY, JANUARY 2, 1963 — 26 PAGES

SIX RESCUED FROM HIDDEN RAVINE

Storm Hampers Search; Cloud Cover Hidden Ravine for Five Days

SANDY, Ore. — Six people trapped in a remote ravine for five days were rescued yesterday in a dramatic operation that had been delayed by heavy cloud cover and snow.

The six, members of a Portland teenage hiking club, had set out on a winter trek December 27th but failed to return as scheduled.

Searchers were unable to spot the concealed ravine from the air due to persistent clouds and snow.

"The weather simply hid that ravine from us," said Sheriff Howard Evans. "It wasn't until yesterday that we got a break in the clouds long enough to locate them."

Stranded for five days — six hikers are rescued from a hidden ravine near Sandy yesterday.
—Oregonian Photo

Helicopter, Ground Crews Combine in Rescue of Six

By DICK HARRISON
Oregonian Staff Writer

A combination of helicopter searches and ground crews finally ended the five-day ordeal of six young hikers missing in the Mount Hood National Forest.

The teens were located by a sheriff's spotter plane shortly after noon yesterday.

"We spotted them and waved the chopper in," said Sheriff Howard Evans. "They were in good spirits, considering everything."

The six were taken by helicopter to a staging area where medics checked them for minor injuries and exposure.

All are expected to recover fully."

TEENAGERS GIVE ALL THE GLORY TO GOD FOR THEIR MIRACULOUS RESCUE

The six teenagers rescued from the hidden ravine near Sandy yesterday have expressed profound gratitude for their survival.

"We want to thank God for watching over us and bringing us through," said one of the teenagers.

Another added, "It was a miracle we were found. We know He was with us every step of the way."

Their families say faith and prayer were a source of comfort during the long days of waiting.

Inside
Search Timeline 2
Survivors' Ordeal 3
Weather Map 2

Chapter 3
Evans Family Feud

There wasn't much to rejoice about at the Evans' home. Solomon Evans was madder than a dog who fell into a hornet's nest. Billy's Dad had never been this upset, absolutely furious, not since he had come to America.

He survived the holocaust and had been blaming God for it ever since. Or shall we say, he denied the existence of God because of it. Either way, the result is the same—a bitter man who doesn't want anything to do with any form of religion.

His logic was sound, certainly not up for debate as far as he was concerned. God didn't exist, and the holocaust was proof that he was right.

How could anyone claim a God was watching over Israel when a Protestant, by the name of Adolf Hitler, was able to convince the German people that all Jews were not humans, worth less than dogs? And then round them up, put them in prison camps, and kill over six million of them, including many children.

Early on, the Jews were marked for annihilation using a golden Star of David. It was Horrible!

Ruth Evans was as much of an atheist as her husband, but really didn't expect Billy to be an exact copy of their lives and beliefs. She was as solid as cement in her anti-God sentiments, for the same reasons as her husband. She escaped the camps because some very kind German sympathizers hid her family in the false walls of their apartment in Berlin. There in the small dwelling place, she developed a disbelief, or to say, she became an atheist.

But her relatives, uncles, aunts, and cousins were not so fortunate. They were shipped to the interior and were never heard from again. It was an intolerable and incomprehensible time in Jewish history, affecting the whole world, plunging it into chaos, fear, and confusion as far as religion was concerned.

Billy was scared but resolved to continue with Christ. He knew the worst was yet to come. His Dad was already a beast. Imagine how he would react when he found out Billy not only believed in God but had also accepted Christ, the Jewish Messiah, as his Savior.

"Maybe you'd better spell it out real clearly to me, Billy," Solomon's anger flashed in his dark Jewish eyes. He called him "Son" when he was in good favor and "Billy" when he was in trouble. "Give me all the facts right now."

Billy ran his fingers through his hair. His hands were shaky, and his mouth was as dry as if he had just wrestled nonstop for ten minutes. He'd told the kids it wouldn't be easy to face his parents. They didn't know how much his Dad hated religion.

Ruth was crying when she returned to the room. She agreed with her husband, but she was a little more liberal. The necessity of all this fuss was beyond her. She couldn't understand why Solomon was so mad about Billy believing in a god that didn't even exist. It seemed ludicrous, absolutely unbelievable.

She wanted to save her family from destruction. "Billy, those kids pressured you into accepting their religion, right? You really didn't know what you were doing. When you've had time to think it over, you'll see what a mistake you made, forget it all, and join us again, right?"

"Ruth," Solomon flushed crimson this time, "I want Billy to answer me. I want all the facts about this trip. You aren't going to hide anything important for us to know." He was pacing the floor and waving his hands all over the place, like an Italian person performing mime.

Mrs. Evans spoke before Billy could answer his Dad. "Billy, you know what the Christians did to our people. Hitler was a Protestant, wasn't he? They were responsible for the torture and murder of over

6,000,000 Jews, many of whom were women and children."

"I know that, Mom, but they weren't real Christians. Their horrible actions have nothing to do with my relationship to Jesus Christ. I'm finally convinced He is the Messiah promised in Isaiah 53." That did it. The cat was out of the bag. Now let's see if Billy can get it back in without getting too scratched up.

The pint-sized wrestler was cringing inside but determined to follow through. He wanted to calm his parents down if possible. "Dad, Mom, take it easy. I'm still Billy Evans, your son. What's all the fuss about? I wasn't pressured into anything.

"I saw God's divine hand in every part of our rescue. There were so many events that couldn't be explained by mere luck. If it were only one, maybe it could be explained away as chance, but multiplied, the odds would've been more than one billion to one that all those things could have happened by pure accident. I know there isn't a gambler in this family. We never played the odds. We always went for the sure thing.

"Dad, Mom, there is NO way to explain the events that had to fall into place to save our lives, my life, your son's life. I argued as long as I could, and every day another part of the jig-saw puzzle was put in place. The extra food Erin brought, Bowie took flying lessons. I was supposed to sit in the front seat. If I had been in the co-pilot's place, we all would be dead now.

"Then Bowie, not even considered a novice, knowing about as much as a rock does about flying a plane, was able to maneuver the aircraft through the ravine with less than one hundred feet to spare on each side.

A thirty-year veteran couldn't have done that, NO WAY.

"Then we had Speedy, our hero pigeon, to save us. Apparently, he was shot on the way back, but he survived, and he saved our lives.

"Imagine that, Dad and Mom, a wounded, brave, one-legged pigeon saved my life." He kept talking as long as he had the floor. This was going to be his only chance to get the whole story told. It was his story, not some author or some radio preacher.

"The minute I admitted that all these circumstances were not just a gambler's lucky day, the minute I stopped trusting in those stupid, worthless worry beads, and the very second I confessed that God existed, the clouds rolled away and the sunshine lit up where we were. It wasn't even two minutes after I agreed that God existed. These facts that I'm telling you HAPPENED TO ME, your son, Blind Billy.

"I had my eyes opened. I may still be blind physically, but I can now see spiritually. Jesus Christ is the Messiah, and I accepted Him as my only and sufficient Lord and Savior, and He will welcome me into His glorious kingdom when I depart this life." There! He said it, now everything was declared after all.

Billy's Dad wasn't convinced. He was getting madder and madder by the minute. "The worst of my nightmares has happened. Now we'll be laughed at by all of our friends. People might even find out we're Jewish. You didn't tell those kids that, did you?"

Billy just hung his head. He wasn't going to lie. His parents correctly interpreted his silence.

"Those brats really got to you, huh, Billy?" Solomon sneered at his son. "I didn't know you were such a weak person. Such a wimp. You caved in when the going got rough. I'm ashamed of you. You betrayed us and all of our ancestors. You're not a Jew. You are a traitor." Solomon was getting to the point of the atomic bomb explosion, and Billy knew it.

Ruth had never seen her husband so furious, absolutely out of control. She knew this wasn't going to end well for their family. Mrs. Evans put her hand on Billy's. "You told them we are Jews. How could you do that? This was a very well-kept family secret!"

Billy took the invisible pulpit again, "I'm not ashamed of my Jewish heritage. We have a lot to be proud of. We gave the world the Bible. As I see it, the whole world is indebted to us; we gave them Jesus Christ. Jesus is the best-known person in the world. He's the most wonderful person who ever lived. He's quoted a thousand

times more than all other famous people put together. His teachings make this world a better place to live."

Every time Billy mentioned Jesus Christ, Solomon Evans became more violent. He clenched his fist and slammed it into the wall, making a hole in the sheet rock big enough to hold a large grapefruit. Billy wasn't sure whether the next swing would be so harmless. "This is getting worse, if that's even possible. You not only believe in God, but you also believe in Christ. Is that what you mean by calling Jesus MY SAVIOR?"

Billy knew he would eventually have to tell them, so it might as well be now. Get the whole drama over with. His Dad certainly couldn't get madder, could he? He might soon find out!

"When we were stranded on the ledge, my eyes were opened. I recognized the mighty hand of God at work on our behalf. When I finally confessed verbally to the rest that I believed in God, the clouds that had hovered over our heads for five days cleared away. It was so awesome, I was scared. It gave me goosebumps, religious goosebumps.

"A pigeon rescued us, a one-legged pigeon that had flown 585 miles in one day. Poor old Speedy died and even had to be rescued from a hungry cat's mouth. Dad, I love you, but I can't deny our rescue was by the hand of Almighty God. I think He did the whole thing to show His love for me, a blind, Jewish, atheist wrestler. I was humbled that HE cared for me enough to put all of us through that drama on the ledge."

Solomon turned to his son and yelled right in his face. "You don't really mean that you have become a fanatic like those other religious jerks, do you? You'll make us the laughing stock of the whole city, or county. I won't have it. Your relatives will be ostracizing us from all the Jewish get-togethers. We'll be alone. I don't like being alone, BILLY!"

The new convert was getting stronger and bolder with each passing moment. It even surprised him. "Dad, I love you and want always to obey you, respecting your wishes. But, there's no way I'm going to turn my back on the Messiah, Who died for me and saved me from my sins."

An almost indescribable contortion came over his dad's face, twisting his manly appearance. He swung back his arm as if to lower the boom on Billy, but Ruth Evans wouldn't have any of this. She stepped in between them and stopped his huge fist from crashing down on Billy, "You'll have to hit me first. I mean it, Solomon. If you hit Billy, I'll leave this house and never return. How could you? He's your only son."

Billy was finally beginning to see that this conversation was becoming hazardous to his health. "Maybe we should all retire now. We can continue this discussion tomorrow, when we've all thought it over and cooled off a bit. Good grief, Dad! It appears that it would have been better if I'd perished in the crash rather than recognize the love of God."

Solomon's eyes were red with anger. "I certainly don't have to recognize anything. I never saw that love. All I ever witnessed was hatred and murder. If there ever was a God, He has completely abandoned our world. I'm giving you a chance to forget this whole thing. You have to decide now, are you going to continue this religious relationship, or are you going to continue living here?"

Mrs. Evans was sobbing. "What are you trying to say, Solomon? Certainly, this religious problem won't destroy this family. I won't hear of it." She was as strong an atheist as Solomon was, but she was also a mother who loved her son more than life itself. She'd never give Billy this ultimatum, NEVER.

"You don't have anything to say about it, Ruth. I want to hear from Billy. Are you going to forget this religion stuff, that despicable Christian junk?"

The tears welled up in Billy's blind eyes. He had only been a Christian for a week, and he was already forced to make a decision that would affect his family, perhaps for the rest of his life. His silence was deafening.

Billy stood up and felt his way out of the kitchen. He didn't want his parents to see the tears of sorrow that were falling down his cheeks. He retreated to his room and slowly closed the door. This was very painful, much more than he ever thought he would feel for anything in life.

When he was gone, Ruth got her chance to defend her son. "Solomon, you know I agree with you about this religion stuff. I don't see any value in it either. I also don't want anyone telling me who the Messiah is, if there even is such a person. But Billy is our only child. We can't turn him away."

"My mind is made up, Ruth," he said icily. "Billy will

have to make a choice. He'll have to give up this stupid religion stuff or find another place to live. I don't want any Bible-reading fanatics around here."

"I can't believe you, Solomon. Why are you acting like a bull in a china shop? I find it impossible to understand why it's all so terrible. Fill me in, please. Perhaps I'm not catching the whole significance. You're going to throw our only son out of his home because he believes in a god that doesn't even exist. This is absolute madness. I'll not stand for it. What makes you so mad IF GOD DOES NOT EVEN EXIST?"

Solomon was even getting belligerent with his wife now. "Your pleading for his cause is of no avail, Ruth. I've made up my mind. If Billy doesn't give up this religion stuff, he's as good as dead as far as I'm concerned."

Ruth was getting mad herself, maybe even desperate. "You're a hard man, Solomon, but I can't believe you're so hard you'd put your own blind son out on the street."

"Don't be so sure, my dear. You really don't know me

that well, then. If you take Billy's side, you can leave too." This angry man, out of control, hater of anything religious, was willing to consider his only son as good as dead because he believed in a god that didn't even exist, AS FAR AS SOLOMON WAS CONCERNED, and he was willing to see the love of his life leave, too. As Ruth said, this is madness.

Ruth was feeling sick to her stomach. That feeling she got when she had heard of the degradation of the prison camps, and was looking at a horrible future. She didn't know why Billy had to be so stubborn. Why couldn't he live his "religion" quietly, as some others did?

She rose, walked out of the kitchen, and went straight to Billy's room. Maybe she could talk him into being a secret disciple. When she knocked on his door, she heard him respond softly, "Come in, Mom."

"How did you know it was me?"

"Well, as mad as Dad is right now, I didn't think it was him. He wouldn't have knocked softly on the door. He's never been the type to seek reconciliation, now has he?"

Ruth sat on Billy's bed and wept bitterly. When he put his arm around her trembling shoulders, she finally calmed down enough to talk. "When we thought you'd crashed in the mountains, we were beside ourselves with grief. Your Dad didn't sleep a wink the whole four days you were missing. He really loves you, Billy. Can't you two work this thing out?"

"I'm not the one who's angry, Mom," he managed to shrug his shoulders. "Just what do you want me to do anyway, abandon my faith, turn my back on the Savior, the Jewish Messiah, Who loved me so much He died in my place?"

Ruth was grasping for straws now. "Couldn't you just be a secret disciple? You know, read your Bible at school and forget going to church, just until you're out on your own."

"Mom, you've always taught me to be assertive, to fight for what I believe in, right? Now you want me to be mediocre about the most important question of the ages—eternal salvation. I can't understand you. I never thought you'd agree to making me a homeless teenager."

She bowed her tired head on Billy's shoulder. "I just want to save my family. Your Dad isn't going to change his mind, Son. This situation is going ... going to get worse. Someone has to give in. Can't it be you?"

"If you only knew what I went through on that mountain. I fought those kids all the way. I gave them every argument I knew. Everything you two taught me, I threw at them, lock, stock, and barrel. They weren't pressuring me. God was revealing Himself to me, there in the crashed Cessna cabin. I found the answer that most of our people have missed for 2000 years. I found the Messiah—Jesus Christ."

She could see she wasn't getting anywhere with her son. How could she? He was just like his parents. When he thought he was right, he'd stick by his guns, no matter what it cost him, even to the edge of the cliff of life. She was proud of him and yet scared to death as well. She knew Solomon would never give in either.

She stood up to leave. "I'll try to do my best for you, Son, but your Dad will never be moved. I'm afraid we're headed for some very sad days. I hope you're able to handle the outcome. I love you, Billy. Good night."

When Ruth closed the bedroom door, she knew the handwriting was on the wall. There would be no peace in this family as long as Billy insisted on keeping his "Savior" and Solomon refused to give up his atheism. She went to bed, knowing she wouldn't sleep a wink that night.

It was a lonely blind wrestler who dug out his Bible, which he had been searching through for six months. He had many questions about following Christ. He'd have to find them himself if his Dad didn't let him go to church.

Where would all this end? He prayed God would be especially close to him in the next few days; they'd be extremely difficult. When he decided to accept Christ, he knew his home life would never be normal again. But he had no way of knowing the depths of hatred and rage his father could muster up against religion, and especially against Christianity and its leader,

Jesus Christ. This was going to get uglier.

He didn't sleep all night. This was going to revolutionize his whole life. He wasn't even sure where he'd be sleeping tomorrow night. He knew he couldn't live on the street.

In the morning, Billy dressed and found his mother in the kitchen. She was still crying. Having not slept all night, she was exhausted and very sensitive. Her eyes were swollen, red, and dark. Billy put his arm on her shoulder. "Don't worry, Mom, things will work out okay, I'm sure of it."

She started to sob so violently that her whole body shook. Billy was her only son. She hugged him. "I don't think you see the gravity of the situation. I think you're too optimistic. Your Dad went to see a lawyer this morning to change our will."

Chapter 4
Nez Perce Twins

Bowie was glad to be back, off the ledge and out of the snow. He wasn't a fan of Big Sky winters. Snow was nice, on calendars and photos, but when you had to change your flat tire in the snow at forty below, the whole idea of "I'm Dreaming of a White Christmas," and snowman things seemed a bit too much.

He'd keep his toes and fingers, thank you. No sense in fighting frostbite and shoveling the white manure if it wasn't necessary. The time on the ledge did nothing but confirm his dislike of the winter wonderland idea. He preferred Western Oregon; the Willamette Valley was perfect for his warm-loving body and soul.

His twin sisters felt differently about the whole ice-and-cold subject. They actually loved the song "Let it Snow" and played it all winter long, hoping it would have some magical effect on the weather. He turned off the worn-out disk every time he passed the Wollensak record player in the living room.

They'd yell at him from their perch upstairs. "Hey there, big guy, quit messing with our minds. We want to make a snowman and put some snow angels in the front yard. Don't you want to plaster us with some big, hard snowballs? We know you do!"

"Don't tempt me, you little twerps, or I'll come up there and bury you under a mountain of pillows. I'm warning you. If you play this song one more time, I'm going to lose my mind, and I know you don't want that to happen, now do you?"

He had threatened to take the record, make a Frisbee out of it, and launch it into space, saying it wouldn't come back until they were out of high school. They both knew that was an idle threat, so they just shrugged it off like water off a duck's back. White Dove loved these banters with Bowie. "Get a life, grappler! We know you like the song, but don't want to admit it."

"Right, I like it about as much as I like a root canal. By the way, how is it going for your selection to the wrestler's cheerleading squad? Do you think there is a possibility that both of you will be chosen?" He hoped they would because he wanted them to be a part of Erin's group at the high school next year. They thought they had as good a chance as the other girls.

What no one knew was that a very determined mother of a classmate wanted this rare privilege for her little daughter. In fact, Monica Wilson was so short she was always given a place at the front of the class, or the teacher wouldn't see her and thus mark her absent. She had to go to the office several times already for being absent when she was actually in the room.

Being small, very small, was the reason she wasn't on any sports team and would never be. Who wanted a four-foot, 60-pound wimp on their team.

The only place she'd ever be able to win a big "L" while in junior high was by joining the marching band or the debate team. BUT, her legs were too short to keep up with the marching requirements, and she couldn't argue her way out of a wet paper bag.

Whenever the neighborhood kids played "Red Rover,"

she was not the last one to be chosen. SHE WAS NEVER CHOSEN. No one wanted someone on their side who passed directly under the outstretched, locked arms. Basketball and volleyball, are you kidding? All she ever did was keep score. She was interested in bowling, but they didn't make balls with finger holes that small, and her family couldn't afford a custom-drilled ball.

The whole family came up short in the height department. The dad, Emmet Wilson, started the problem off by mustering up only three feet and eleven inches. He wanted a job as a policeman, but the only division they'd even consider him for was traffic control. He could be one of the greatly admired patrolmen who gave out parking and jaywalking tickets to happy-go-lucky Lebanonese (citizens of Lebanon, Oregon, of course).

But even that was a challenge. He had to come up to at least four feet in stockings to get the job. First, he went to a chiropractor and underwent a stretch machine treatment. It consisted of a brace around the chin and neck with accompanying clamps on his feet.

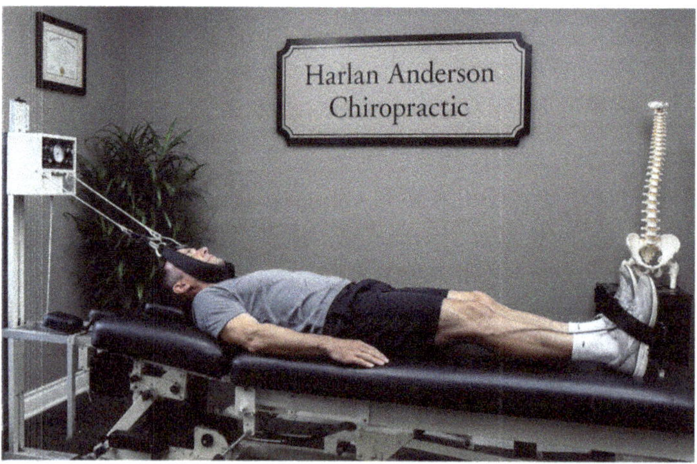

It pulled about every fifteen seconds. This torturous experience gained him 3/4 of an inch if he got down to the station and was measured within one hour.

He was still 1/4 of an inch short. He was desperate for work; any job would do. This particular employment had great benefits, including dental and eye glasses. Just before the time to measure, he put on extra-thick socks, spent an hour on the stretch machine, then took a hammer and pounded on the top of his head until a little swollen ball appeared.

Running quickly into the police station, he asked Sergeant Kochian to measure him right away. IT WORKED! He was exactly four feet. He was hired. The kind Sergeant wanted to know if he needed a few days off to recover from a sore spot on the top of his head. He said he'd be fine, show him to the tailor so he could get his nice, new, blue uniform made to fit.

Monica was very happy for her dad. Now they could buy a VW bug, as it was the only car he could see over the steering wheel. She had her own challenges. Dialing the combination on her locker was not a problem. It was reaching the top shelf that aggravated her. Finally, she asked the teacher in the wood shop to make her a step stool so she could use the upper shelf. He gladly did it for her.

Because Monica's mother, Mary, was called Pintsize Wilson, she took this opportunity for her daughter to be a cheerleader very seriously. She felt that if Monica didn't make the squad, it would scar her emotionally for the rest of her life. This is exactly why she was taking matters into her own hands.

The last tryout was scheduled for the next afternoon.

Since she worked on the serving line in the cafeteria, she conjured up a diabolical plan of getting rid of the competition. As the other contestants stood in front of her, Sandra secretly sprinkled X-Lax powder on their mashed potatoes. She thought the girls would definitely miss the tryouts.

But what was this new development? The Pinetree twins didn't eat at the school that day. "Where are those brats, anyway?" she asked the lady serving the green beans, who thought the potato lady was being a little cruel and strange, to say the least!

White Dove and Running Fawn missed the fourth hour and lunch because they both had appointments with their favorite dentist. Dr. Lionel Payne. Being the absolute clowns that they were, the Nez Perce twins made a lot of jokes about his last name. "Oh, how dreadful! I have to be in Dr. Payne's office all afternoon." or "Don't worry, Dr. Payne, I won't cry if it hurts."

Of course, they didn't say these things to his face, and why would they? He still had the pliers and the noisy drill in HIS hands, didn't he? They may have been lacking in mental worth, but they weren't dumb, as Bowie always remarked about them.

Since the Pinetree twins and Monica were the only ones to show up for the tryouts, they got the cheerleading roles for this wrestling season. The judge thought it was strange that the other ten girls didn't appear. She knew they all were dead set on winning the coveted position.

The junior high, like any well-run public school in the USA, had many health policies. If just two kids had digestive problems after lunch, the health superintendent, Dan Castle, came running as soon as possible. It was considered a major threat. Ten girls being sick right after lunch was a catastrophe! It had never happened before, not in any of the district's 29 schools.

Upon much investigation, it was found that the only thing all ten had in common on their stainless steel trays was mashed potatoes with bacon chips on the top. So the spud was the culprit. The next thing the homespun detective discovered was that all ten girls missed cheerleading tryouts. This was too much of a coincidence as far as the amateur Sherlock was concerned.

There was something rotten in Denmark, for sure. Dan put two and two together and identified a supposed guilty party. All he had to do was find out WHO actually showed up for the competition: only Monica and the Pinetree twins. Since Monica's mother was the one serving mashed potatoes on the line, she was called into the principal's office. They went to her locker and found five empty boxes of powdered X-Lax.

Man, was this spud lady in deep trouble. Who'd have thought a simple cheerleading elimination would bring out such a diabolical plan like this? Mary Wilson was not admitting to anything, but the evidence was too overwhelming. They dismissed her on the spot and told her that if she thought it was unfair, she should get herself a good lawyer.

As she was walking out the door, Mr. Castle told her not to leave town. He thought the health department might be sending the police to her house for a more detailed discussion of the horrid matter. She cleaned out her locker and went home, stopping at the *Lebanon Express* to ask for the page listing the local employment opportunities. She was no quitter, never had been.

When the whole story would eventually leak out, as gossip does, Monica would be absolutely horrified. How was she ever going to live down this scandal? Being called shorty was already a terrible burden to carry. She could imagine what horrible jokes she'd be the brunt of for the rest of the year, maybe the rest of her high school days. Some might even think she had something to do with it.

The kind principal didn't think for one minute that Monica was involved in the scheme. To prove it, he called her into his office the following day. "Listen, my friend, I know for certain you had nothing to do with his whole sordid mess. Therefore, I'm allowing you to remain on the cheerleading squad, if you want to.

"Just be on the alert, this crime your mother committed still has to be dealt with by the proper authorities. I know you're going to get a lot of harassment here at school. I can only do a certain amount of policing in that area. BUT, I'll do as much as I can for you.

"Just be brave and hang in there. We're all pulling for you." With that encouragement, the kind principal dismissed Monica and followed her out of the office. Mrs. Sue Baine was only one of the staff members who already knew about the whole ordeal. The compassionate mom started clapping for Monica as she went through their area. The rest, thinking it was a nice thing to do, followed suit.

The first meeting of the cheerleaders was a bit sparse. Mr. Castle, the kind and fair Linn County superintendent, insisted that all ten victims get another opportunity to try out once they recovered completely. But these three were not going to be cut, no matter what happened. Bowie's sisters were extremely happy to have Shortie on their squad. She'd be the one to stand up tall at the top of their pyramid. How 'bout that?

Chapter 5
Homeless Billy Evans

The number-one topic of gossip on the Lebanon Union High School (LUHS) campus was the Cessna crash and the ensuing rescue. At a special assembly, principal, Earl B. Wise, allowed the survivors to describe in detail the tragedy that turned into a divine victory.

Erin's voice broke a little when she mentioned the tremendous sacrifice of a small pigeon. "We found a few shotgun pellets in his body, which gave us the impression that some bird-hater shot him. But Speedy prodded on. With only one leg to take off on, he flew the rest of the way, and we all owe our lives to the little pigeon that God gave a beaming gift to."

The second item of conversation was the whereabouts of the eight-foot anaconda. Since it had disappeared from the glass cage in the biology room, no one had seen it.

Shane had found some eggs on the wrestling mats. Mr. Brown, the science teacher, carefully guarded the eggs. "We want to increase the size of the snake family at LUHS."

"Thrills a minute," Erin wailed. "All we need is more slimy, ugly reptiles crawling around the building." When God put enmity between the woman and the snake, he must have had Erin in mind. Anything that slithers and gets within striking range of her definitely has a death wish.

Billy brought his troubles to school with him. "You can't believe how angry my Dad was last night. According to what Mom said, he'd have lowered the boom on me, literally, if she hadn't gotten between us, literally. He's talking to a lawyer right now to change the family will. I'm afraid to go home after school."

The kids ate lunch together in the cafeteria and afterward met in the 57' Chevy to have a time of prayer. Marty was deeply concerned for his Jewish friend, as were all of them. "We have no idea how far your Dad is going with this matter. We can't promise you anything but the presence of the Holy Spirit and the peace of God as you choose to follow Christ."

Erin put her right hand over her heart like she was trying to keep it from beating so hard it would explode out of her chest and fall on the car floor. "It won't be easy, Billy," Erin tried to comfort him. "But God is with you. He'll give you strength and wisdom."

Her eyes became cloudy, contemplating the situation Billy was in. She also thanked God that she never had to face such a problem at home. Being raised in a Christian home, where Jesus was always the priority, was a tremendous blessing. This was a gift from God, and she knew it and often told everyone she could.

They all prayed in turn. When it came to Billy, he was crying.

> God, I love my parents, and I need my home. I can't deny my faith in Christ. I owe everything to Him. Please help me heal the wounds at my house. I'm trusting in Jesus' name. Amen.

There were more moist eyes in the car.

When Billy went back into the school building, the others had another meeting. Marty wanted to do something, but nobody seemed to know what could be done. "This is going much further than I could've imagined. I can't understand hatred so strong it would turn a person against his only son, blind even."

"I've been a Christian for only a few years," Erin added. "I've never seen such antagonism against a new convert. Do you think Billy has the stamina to follow through with his faith?" Her heart felt for the pint-sized grappler. She put his name at the top of her prayer list.

Bowie didn't like the looks of the whole matter. "When I told my parents I had accepted Christ, they weren't glad or mad. I think they're still waiting to see if it was going to make a difference in my life." Bowie knew that words would mean nothing to his parents. They wanted to see whether he would control his anger and change his speech patterns. And he did.

Travis Pinetree declared that he had observed this very sudden change in his rodeo-riding son. "Bowie, I'm amazed at how much your life has changed since you started following the white man's God. Maybe there's something to this religion after all."

Bowie tried to explain that it wasn't just "following a religion," it was being "born again," and He wasn't just the "white man's God" but the Savior of the whole world. Jesus is also the Savior of the Native Americans. His admiring parents listend to his words, but they fell on unbelieving ears.

Shane was probing his friend's testimony. "And it has made a difference, hasn't it, Bowie?"

"It sure has. I don't have much interest in some of the old things that used to occupy my thoughts so much. I'm happy to attend church. I find the Bible interesting and a guide for my daily life. I don't curse anymore, and I try to treat my sisters with kindness. Even my Mom says she can see a difference in my actions. I guess being around you do-gooders has had a positive effect on me."

Shane smiled at the Nez Perce, who had become such a good friend. He remembered the first time they met. Bowie would impress anyone with his size and friendly mannerisms. Here was a kid who was allowed to recognize and take pride in his heritage, something Billy couldn't do. "Apparently, Billy is going to be disinherited and thrown out of his own home if he continues to follow Christ," Marty said. "He has a situation that's light-years more difficult than Erin and I have ever had. What will he do if he's kicked out of his home?"

Erin was thinking about the consequences of Solomon's decisions, "This idea of hiding the fact that he's a Jew is only going to get Billy's Dad in some tough situations when the community finds out. I can't see the value of what he's been doing all these years. No one I know here in Linn County has any reason to hate Jews. There's no antisemitism here. Have his parents seen the large plaque in the city library with all the names of the residents of Linn County who died liberating the Jews from those horrible concentration camps?"

Erin was right. Many Linn County citizens served in WWII. They delivered France and marched across Europe with George Patton to Berlin, meeting the

British General Montgomery. Together, they routed the disorganized Germans and closed all the concentration camps. They freed the Jewish people and let them return home, many coming to the USA as immigrants. There was no anti-Semitism in Linn County. Solomon was making a big mistake by hiding his heritage.

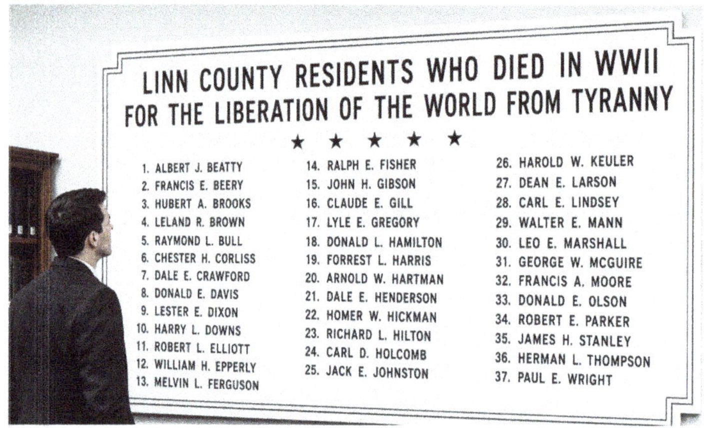

******

It's never easy on the LUHS mat the first day back from Christmas vacation. Bodies are out of shape and flabby. Coach Hazewinkel patted Bowie on the midsection. "You're not in bad shape for the shape you're in."

Shane and Marty started out working together. Marty was very excited. "I missed the workouts, the calculations of losing weight, and putting on the plastic clothes to sweat it off. I really like this sport."

Shane was just as excited, but not for the same reasons. "Personally, I think you are a sadist," Shane blew out as he was trying to catch his breath, "or masochist, perhaps both." I love this sport because it thrills me to have my hand raised in victory. That winning feeling is great, especially when you know it was all depending on you. But losing weight isn't one of my favorite parts of this sport. At times, I wish I wrestled heavyweight like Bowie and could eat what I want when I want."

Marty didn't agree with Shane, "Did you notice the heavyweights don't score many points. They can't shoot for a single-leg takedown. If they did, the other wrestler would sprawl, putting his opponent on the mat, with him on top. I prefer to be able to make any move I want at any time I want and end up on TOP." Marty had made a habit of being on top, and his opponents hated wrestling him because of it.

The Warriors had a fairly young team, riding a 4-2 record to the top of the conference. Bowie was pushing his weight around on the far mat. He yelled at everyone to stop and listen to him. "We have a chance to win the conference. It also looks like we have a good enough team to place high in the state, with a few champions, right?" He got only affirmative yells and screams from some hyped-up wrestlers.

Englebert Farnsworth III was really overweight. He'd spent the Christmas holiday in the Bahamas, sipping lemonade and eating barbecue every night. He had to lose 12 pounds in two days. How was he going to do it?

He still insisted on wrestling Shane as if his life depended on it. That was acceptable to the Lacombite; it made him more aggressive. Shane was either wrestling defensively against Marty or fighting for mere survival with Bert.

Since Shane had beaten Bert in a wrestle-off just before the vacation break, the banker's son hadn't been such a threat. Shane knew he could be victorious again, demand Bert's weight class, and push him off the team. But that didn't interest him. He wasn't the vengeful type, and the team needed Bert at that weight class.

Coach Hazewinkel took Marty, Shane, Bowie, and Billy off to the side after practice. "You guys have a great chance to be regional champs. You're all good enough to make a dent in the state finals, too. There are two areas you must improve, though. You have to get better at your escapes and more aggressive with your takedowns.

"As far as the escapes go, the best method is either a reversal or a standup. If you're going to stand up, it's better to back into your opponent and look for a standing switch or a return drop switch. We've got to work on these. I'm talking about 100 times each practice session. No time for fooling around now."

After practice, the wrestlers met Erin in the parking lot. The Woods kid had still been keeping a close watch on his car, as some of the students weren't at all happy with Shane and his crew's popularity. He retained the thin string tied from his hood ornament to the grill. This would warn him if anyone messed around with his motor.

Erin loved to start the powerful V-8 engine. She was just a hot-rodder at heart. She loved the roar of the motor and the smell of the hot engine. Usually, she'd rev up the motor until Shane insisted that she back off. That's exactly what she was doing when he noticed the string was broken.

"Turn it off, Erin," Shane tried to get her attention. Finally, he hammered on the hood with his fist. Erin flinched, backed off from the steering wheel, and just stared at him, wide-eyed and lower lip quivering. This was her favorite way to make anyone think they'd hurt her sensitive feelings. Shane was not moved.

"Quit your whimpering," he screamed over the roar of the engine. "Just shut it off." He gestured by running his palm across his Adam's apple. She finally got the point.

While the motor came to a stop, Shane opened the hood. There before his eyes was a sight that would chill the spine of anyone with a sensitive nose: strips of Limburger cheese lay across all the pipes of the exhaust manifolds.

Putting stinky Limburger cheese on the motor would stink up the whole motor area. Every time the area got hot, the disgusting smell would return. Sometimes the lingering stench would force a motor replacement.

Bowie sauntered up, looked at the motor, and whistled. “The old Limburger-cheese-on-the-manifold trick. You’re lucky you caught it in time. If that cheese had melted, you wouldn’t be able to drive the car again without changing your manifold. Man, you really do have some guys around here who don’t like you, right?”

Shane and Bowie promptly removed the almost-melted, smelly substance and threw it in the garbage. Billy was smelling the cheese. “Man, how can anyone eat this horrible stuff? It smells much worse than skunk weed.” The kids had offered to give Billy a ride home. His Dad usually came by to pick him up, but somehow they knew he wouldn’t be there tonight.

There was a stop at the Lebanon Police station. The kids wanted to give Sergeant Kochian the information they had obtained at the airport in Boise, Idaho. The sergeant was always glad to see these kids. He often said that if all the teens at LUHS had just half of the deportment of those students, his job would be much easier.

“So you think Ron Thomas isn’t dead,” the sergeant conjectured. “An interesting theory. I wasn’t here when the crime occurred. Let me look into the facts and the possibilities. I’ll get back to you. We might need more information and some material witnesses. Is there any possibility you could be wrong?”

Shane really liked this police officer. "You should've seen his face when I called him by his real name. He got so nervous that he even quit work after only a week on the job. No, there's not one chance in a million that I'm wrong."

The good sergeant was always giving these teens the attention they deserved, but he never failed to warn them not to try to do the job he and his men were trained and paid to do. Marty always assured him they wouldn't overstep their boundaries or usurp his authority. At least that's what they always intended to do.

The kids drove Billy to his nice home on Rose Street. When they pulled into the driveway, Erin noticed something. "You must have some visitors, Billy. There are a bunch of suitcases stacked on the front porch."

"We weren't scheduled to have any," the lightweight wrestler commented. "Wait a minute. What color are the suitcases?"

"They're a matched set covered with brown leather," Erin answered quickly. "Just like the one you took on the trip ..." She realized the obvious. She couldn't finish the sentence. Her stomach was in a knot, and she looked at the rest of the gang in the car. It wasn't a pleasant sight, his luggage on the porch. Suddenly, her stomach was caught in her throat.

Billy was apparently very nervous. "Does each suitcase have white metal latches and hinges with black handles, Erin?"

"That's right, Billy. Do you know the people who own the suitcases?" She was hoping her conclusions were all wrong, praying they were. She couldn't imagine the turmoil the little Jewish wrestler must have been going through at this moment.

There was a long pause, and then Billy spoke with fear in his voice. "I ... I ... I think those are my suitcases. Could you kids wait here for a minute while I find out what's going on?"

Billy climbed out of the car with his head spinning. He

entered gingerly into the house and heard his Mom weeping as she sat on the expensive leather sofa. "What's going on, Mom? Why are my suitcases sitting on the front porch?" Billy was afraid of what he was going to hear.

Ruth Evans wasn't able to speak for a while. She just wept bitterly. When she finally got control of herself, she asked Billy to sit down on the sofa beside her. "There's no containing your dad's anger. He finished with the lawyer and has packed your clothes. He said I was to give you one more chance to stop all this religious fanaticism. If you won't, then you're no longer our son, and you can't stay in this home even one more night."

Until now, Billy had been plenty scared, but at least a little bit optimistic. Now he was destroyed. He breathed deeply and prayed silently, "Where do I go from here, Lord? I decided to follow you, and now I'm homeless. I need your presence and power right now."

The blind wrestler looked straight at his mom's face, "I

knew the situation was serious, but not deadly. I can't give up my faith in Christ; it's all I've ever dreamed of having—a strong faith in a Living Hope. I can't turn back now. Jesus left his home in glory, was rejected, beaten, and suffered a horrible death so I could live with Him in heaven forever if I asked Him to come into my heart and save me. I did ask Him, and I'll be with Him eternally. I want the same thing for you and Dad, Mom."

"Your Dad loves you, Billy, but he'll not have any religion in this house. I tried my best to change his mind. He's as stubborn as you are. Why won't one of you give in? You both are breaking my heart and ruining our family."

Billy was facing a test many spiritual giants have never had to experience. "It's not a matter of being just as stubborn as Dad. I've found eternal life in Jesus Christ, the Messiah, and I can't go back."

"But, Billy," his Mom pleaded with him, "you're blind, how will you get along. Please, please reconsider your decision to be a Christian. Is following Christ worth losing your inheritance and being thrown out of your home? I can't believe that following a religious leader who died almost 2,000 years ago is worth all of this. This all seems to be incomprehensibly stupid."

"Mom," Billy placed his hand on her shoulder, "that's because you're not understanding the seriousness of the situation. Jesus was much more than a religious leader. He claimed and proved He was the Son of God by raising people from the dead. He is Jehovah in the flesh. The whole Old Testament is chocked full of clear prophecies relating to His arrival on earth and His ministry, including His horrible and unfortunate death."

She was incredulous, "You didn't learn all this on that trip out east, I know that for sure. Were you studying these things in secret before you went on the trip?" She came to this conclusion after finding a Bible and other religious books in Braille.

The pint-sized grappler was amazed at his mom's perception of the whole ordeal, "Wow, Mom, you're quite a detective. Yes, I've been studying the New Testament on my own long before I made the trip. I was comparing the facts of Jesus' life with the prophecies in the Old Testament."

"We Jews have always believed the Old Testament, haven't we? For Pete's sake, WE wrote it, all of it! Even the New Testament. You know this, don't you? The Apostles were Jews; the early Christians were Jews. Not all Jews have been atheists, and not all Jews have rejected Christ. Many have been born again and have received Him as their Lord and Messiah. For this, they were killed, even at the hands of Jewish religious leaders. Stephen, the deacon, was the first one."

Ruth made it clear, "Maybe a lot have become Christians, but your dad and I haven't. We believe in evolution, not in creation. The whole religious saga never interested us and still doesn't. We see no reason to come to the conclusions you have. Really, then the trip wasn't the first time you had considered all of these things. Huh, this is news to me, but I did have my suspicions. What made you start studying these nonsensical things?"

"Well, my best friends are very strong believers in the Bible as the Word of God and Jesus as God's Son. They've all made decisions to follow Christ, no matter what it costs them. I've been noticing the way they act, their demeanor, and their conversations. I found out they're not just fanatical, they're logical, and they definitely practice what Jesus taught in the Bible. He called it the greatest commandment."

He wanted to read it from the Bible, but thought it wasn't wise to do so right now. So he quoted it verbatim, "*Love the Lord thy God with all your heart, all your mind, and all your soul and love your neighbor as yourself.* Jesus said this was the whole law in one sentence."

Ruth didn't believe all of this. "Where did you get all of this information, being blind and all, just out of that braille Bible I found in your room?" She was being a little degrading to her own son!

"I borrowed the Braille Bible from the school library. I brought home only one book at a time. Studying over the last six months has helped me reach my own conclusions. But, it wasn't JUST the Bible reading. The trip also helped me put those conclusions into an act of faith in Jesus Christ that gave me eternal life. Of that, I'm absolutely sure!"

Ruth was almost finished, "Your dad and I have sacrificed a lot to give you the kind of life that could put you on a road to success, even though you're blind. Now you're about to throw all of our hopes and dreams into the gutter with this religious stuff. It's unbelievably ungrateful on your part."

"I was born physically blind, and for years I've followed your beliefs, living in spiritual blindness. Now I'm still physically blind, but spiritually I see, and Who I see with my heart will guide me, of that I'm confident. I'll always love you two."

With that, he hugged and kissed his heartbroken mother and walked out the door to the '57 Chevy. "Will you guys help me put my luggage in the car? I've just been thrown out of my own home!"

Chapter 6
A Visit to the Prison

Jesus Christ said that belief in Him would cause fathers to turn against their sons. He certainly had Billy's situation in mind. The kids didn't know exactly what to do with the cast-out, so they took him home with them to Rocking L Ranch.

Mr. and Mrs. Lynch could hardly believe Solomon Evans would be so cruel to his own son. Edna Lynch had a mother's heart, for any child, "You should phone your mother, Billy, so she won't worry about where you are. You can stay here with us until we can find a solution to your problem."

The Lynches had already discussed this possibility and reached an agreement. This was their way of having a happy marriage. They had to agree on something, or it wasn't done or purchased. This wasn't a difficult decision. They didn't take much time to decide that their spare bedroom would be Billy's if he were thrown out of his home. Their home was his home as long as it was necessary. God would provide everything they needed to do this. They had all the promises they needed to make this decision easy.

After he phoned his mother, the three grapplers meandered out to Marty's wrestling room. They sat there looking at Billy like Job's friends did. What a pitiful situation Billy found himself in tonight. But they were determined not to let the little guy be the main attraction at a pity party.

Shane took over the situation. "Let's have a word of prayer, and then we can work on our escapes and takedowns, as Coach Hazewinkel suggested." That sounded like a good idea, so they did it with great enthusiasm, followed by huffs and puffs.

The takedowns were fast and furious. There was always an aggressor and a passive wrestler. The passive guy would only resist about fifty percent, allowing the aggressor to follow through with the move. When the aggressive wrestler wanted to go full hilt, he gave the word. Then it was every man for himself.

Round-robin wrestling is when the winner or loser stays in the circle, or they take turns. Billy was giving it all he had. He was taking his frustrations out on his friends. They couldn't contain his bold attacks. At the end of one hour, they were exhausted, soaking wet, and a lot better wrestlers. Having Billy living at the ranch was just what they needed to hone their skills for the regional and state tournaments.

Shane could see they were gaining ground. "We ought to do this every night. We're going to win that state championship trophy, aren't we?"

While the boys were battling it out on the mat, Mr. Lynch was on the phone with Solomon Evans. By the tone of Fred's voice, Mrs. Lynch could tell the conversation was not producing any fruit. "But Solomon, surely you can't throw a 16-year-old kid out on his own, especially when he's blind."

"Don't tell me what I can't do," Solomon was adamant. "I'll do what I think is best for my household, you take care of your own, okay?"

When Fred hung up the phone, he was red in the face. "Maybe Solomon doesn't realize it, but there are legal penalties for people who throw their kids out on the street. I know we could ruin his jewelry business if we wanted to run this story in the paper."

Erin was listening to the whole conversation. "Surely, you won't do that, will you, Daddy? I don't think Billy would approve of that kind of action against his parents. Can't we work out something else for him? This is God's doing; He has some plan for Billy."

"Billy is welcome to stay here as long as he needs to, but I don't think we should plan on adopting him. Do you know what I mean?"

Erin nodded affirmatively. "I know exactly what you mean. We need to pray about this and expect God to work something out for poor Billy. I certainly am glad I'm not in his shoes. I thank God for my parents every day." With that, she rushed over to both of them and gave them the bear hug of the month. She wasn't kidding about how thankful she was, and everyone would soon know it.

There was a terrific turmoil building up in Billy's soul. Where would he go? What would he do? How could he support himself? Would his Dad continue ostracizing him from the family—forever? All these questions were running through his head like a speeding train, nowhere to go, nowhere to rest, and nowhere to stop.

"Certainly God has some plan for me," Billy tried to

explain to the others as they walked back to the house. "Don't you think so, Shane? He isn't going to leave me high and dry, is He?" Billy's new faith was based on the Bible, but he knew so little of its contents. So, in a manner of speaking, his faith was as large as his knowledge of the promises in the Word of God, which he knew needed to be increased.

Shane felt deeply for his Jewish friend. There'd have to be an answer for him, an answer only God could provide. "We trusted God completely when we were stranded on the ledge. He proved trustworthy there, and He's still faithful, in every area. We have to trust, Billy, that's our only recourse."

"I know I have little faith because I have very little Bible training. I suppose that with more time spent in the Bible and greater knowledge of its promises, my faith will grow. I believe this is what the Apostles meant when they said, 'Increase our faith', don't you?"

"I believe you're on to a very basic rule in spiritual growth. I've been trying that formula and have found it to be just as accurate as you claim. Pastor Ballentine has been discipling me, and I'd like to invite you to join us. It'd be great for you and for me."

The next day, after wrestling practice, the Chevy wound its way up the freeway to the State Prison in Salem.

Shane, Marty, and Billy wanted to visit Shane's ex-neighbor, who had been there for five years. When they got an audience with Mark Traker, he was surprised to see them.

Mark put his right hand on the narrow table in front of the thick glass and talked on the phone. "Of all the people to visit me, you'd have been the last on my list. To what do I owe this great pleasure? Mine is a lonely lot here."

Shane tried to act normally. He stared through the three-inch-thick glass and talked via the telephone receiver in his hand. “There’s no shadow of a doubt, I saw Ron Thomas at the airport in Boise, Idaho. He was alive and well. What do you think about that?”

Mark raised his eyebrows and looked around him. He also managed a smile. His discretion was apparent. “Of course, I’ve always known I was innocent. If we could get some pictures of him, or even better, capture him, I could finally prove I didn’t kill him. So, that rascal didn’t have enough sense to stay hidden. He must be hard up for cash.”

Shane continued with his good news. “I’ve notified Sergeant Kochian. He’s the new man in charge of Linn County. He’s also a personal friend who said he’d begin looking into the matter. I hope we can do something for you. I can’t imagine being locked up here for five years when you’re innocent. I thought one week was awful.”

Mark was getting so excited that it was hard to contain himself. “There’s another way that this case could be busted wide open. Since Ron Thomas isn’t dead, his coffin must be empty. If you could get permission to exhume the body, we could at least prove he wasn’t dead. Do you think that’s even a possibility?” He was so enthusiastic, he almost spilled his cup of water.

“That sounds like a possibility, Mark,” Shane tried to encourage him. “I’ll talk to my friends, and we’ll see what we can do for you.”

Prison life leaves a lot to be desired. The hardened criminal isn’t anyone’s choice of best friends. Some have been released, and it only took them a month to return. Others returned to their old ways and, within a few weeks, were ushered into the presence of their Creator, the Judge of all humanity.

Some criminals found a motive to square away and never returned. These were supported by loving family members who cared enough to make a wonderful difference.

Others who never returned give the credit to finding Christ while behind bars.

The difference between these groups is that some found a way to change their wicked ways, gaining freedom until they passed over the Jordan to meet their Maker, unprepared for the encounter. The other was redeemed from their many sins, gaining salvation that was good until they crossed the Jordan, to be joyfully received by their Creator and Savior into eternal life.

Before Shane left, he asked Mark if he could pray for him. His response was interesting. "Shane, I've never been a religious man. Do you think God would be interested in my case now? It seems like I'd only be trying to impress the man upstairs. It would be kind of like a foxhole prayer, don't you think, Shane?"

Shane responded. "My Great Uncle George Moore III was an Army sergeant who stormed Normandy Beach on June 6, 1945. It was a horrible experience. He told me that when he got past the beach part and up onto the slope, he had to dig a foxhole. "The shells were coming fast and close. He knew the platoon was in trouble. He'd never been a religious man, but he thought this would be a good time to start! He prayed to God, Jehovah, the Creator of all things. My uncle wanted God to give them some air support, at least enough to reach the base of the hill in front of them.

"He even sent me his prayer. I memorized it.

> Oh Mighty God, the Jehovah of the Jewish people. We are here, in Germany, to liberate Your people, Your children, from the hands of a madman. We need to take this beach. Please, Lord, send us air support so we can march to Berlin and empty those evil, horrible, murderous concentration camps.

"One of the Navy's pilots hit a German plane right above them. The Luftwaffe pilot came in low over their heads, hit the beach right in front of their position, and plowed a ditch for them, right up to the base of the mountain. George thought it was interesting that

God used the enemy's plane to resolve their problem. Later, he became a fervent Christian.

"The point I'm trying to make, Mark, is that God is the Controller of all things, including our situations. He can use many people and various circumstances to give us what we need or want. The enemy of our souls owns a thousand cattle. Our God owns all the hills where all the earth's cattle graze. Are you getting my point?"

Mark was smiling now. "Okay, let's ask for some help from above. We'll really need it." After Shane prayed, he said goodbye and promised not to let any grass grow under his feet.

Chapter 7
Locate a Headstone

Shane's promise to Mark Traker was not an idle one. But he wasn't the law and didn't want to see an irate police sergeant. He decided it was best to stop at the police station and get his friend's opinion. He took Marty and Billy with him. As they strolled into the station, the radio was screeching and crackling with static. "It's not a good night for radio signals," Patrolman Ron Hinds informed them. Did you want to see the sergeant? If so, you'll have to go to the Centwise Drug Store. It was robbed about half an hour ago."

After they left, the new patrolman started chatting with the secretary. "What is it with these kids from Lacomb? The sergeant treats them like they were his own children. I've never seen anything like it in my whole life."

Rebecca Thibaudeau, the long-time secretary, had some answers for him. "That Shane Woods came here in June. He was involved in a scrimmage with the Snow Peak robbers. It was a crime that greatly concerned our immediate family. My Uncle Jeff met his end from some thugs stealing dynamite from the logging camp.

"For the whole summer, they've been involved in other

problems facing our community. They remind me of the kids in 'The Hardy Boys' books. I read all of them, you know. The sergeant is thankful they're proactive on our behalf. Hey, if all the kids at LUHS had their attitude, we'd probably have half as much work around here. These kids are as wise as owls and as harmless as doves."

The grapplers zoomed over to Centwise Drug Store just in time to find their favorite bully quivering in his brat boots. It appeared that the robber knew him personally and made several nasty threats to his whole immediate family. Engelbert Farnsworth III was visibly shaken and scared. "I ... I ... saw ... his eyes through the holes in his mask. He looked serious when he threatened my family."

The first thing that came to Shane's type "A" personality was an elated feeling of "How does it feel to be on the receiving end of a bully's tirade?" But that's not what came out of his mouth. "Man, Bert, that must've been scary. I hope he's not making plans on following through with those evil threats."

For the first time since Shane knew him, Bert, the teenage president of the local bully and brat club, was without words. He just stared at the Lacombites like they were from outer space. Then the rich kid turned and went to the back of the store to put a cold, wet rag on his hot forehead.

Sergeant Kochian couldn't figure it out. "It doesn't make sense to me. Why would anyone rob this store? It carries very little money in the till. There's even a sign right in front saying that very thing." He pointed to a professionally printed sign that read, "Till always emptied every hour on the hour."

"Then money wasn't the reason. He stopped by here to harass Bert," Marty commented.

Billy's wheels were turning fast. "Hey, that's it! He wanted to harass Bert. But why? That's the question. He certainly did a good job of getting the LUHS bully scared out of his wits.

"The only link we have with Bert is the wrestling team. Maybe he's on a vendetta against the team. During the first wrestle-offs, who was cut from the team? They were Albert Franz, Tommy Lee, and Frankie Thomas.

I was standing behind them when they got the bad news. Hey, that's it. Frankie Thomas must be related to Ron Thomas. And I bet John was the robber here."

The Sergeant was duly impressed. "Wow, since Billy joined your junior detective club, your skills of deduction have increased tenfold. So, Dick Tracy, you've concluded that Ron Thomas robbed this store?"

"Revenge seems logical to me. He couldn't have taken more than $35, according to Bert. It looks like the school bully is getting some of his own medicine. I'm a little tickled to see this happen.

"Bert hasn't stopped harassing us since Shane and Marty met him in June. His animosity against us is known all over town. I hope John doesn't follow through with his threats against Bert and his family. I do think he's mean enough to do so."

"Billy, why don't you come to the station after school, and we can give you a job answering the radio or something. It's a shame to let a mind with such good deductive powers sit around and do nothing. I'm not kidding. I know Shane works at the T.P. Oil Company. Could you work the same hours for us, then catch a ride home with him?"

"Hey! I got a job. Who would've guessed that?"

Shane was happy for his blind wrestling friend. "No problem here, Sergeant. I'll drop him off after school tomorrow, and you can pick his brain. Try to leave enough grey matter for him to pass his classes and stay at least one IQ point ahead of Harriet, our orangutan friend!"

The threesome decided to take a stroll through

the cemetery to the Ron Thomas grave stone. The sergeant said he'd been buried there. The caretaker was mowing the grass for the last time this year. It had already started getting a little brown at the very tips.

Ty Bond was the man riding the Yard Machine, the new sit-down lawn mower the city had purchased recently. It was a really good job, sitting down while one is mowing. The caretaker saw them and waved, indicating he'd catch them on the next pass. When he shut off the engine, he jumped down and blurted out, "Did you know I was given a job with 1,232 people under me?"

"What do you mean, Ty? Do you have a supervisor's job somewhere else? If so, what in the world are you doing this mowing for?" Marty wanted to know.

"No, it's THIS JOB. Don't you get it? I have 1,232 people UNDER me, here, in the ground. Man, it ruins a joke when you have to explain it to lunkheads."

All three of them smiled to make him feel better. They thought the joke was a little corny, though. Shane pointed to the center of the cemetery. "We want to see the grave site of Ron Thomas. He was buried here five years ago. Do you know where it's located?"

"Yes, I do, but the deceased Ron Thomas has some serious legal problems."

Billy was scratching his head. “LEGAL PROBLEMS! Are you spoofing us? What kind of legal problems could a dead person have?”

“Not John himself, of course not. It’s just that the previous caretaker was dating the whiskey bottle a little too much, if you know what I mean. He made a mistake and buried John in the wrong place. The headstone says OLGA McINTOSH SNODGRASS, but the coffin six feet down holds the unfortunate remains of your friend Ron Thomas.”

Marty was quick to correct the uninformed caretaker. “Ron’s no friend of ours. He’s a thief and just robbed the Centwise drug store in town.”

“Now YOU are trying to be funny. How can a dead man rob a store?”

“That’s what we’re trying to tell you, Ty,” Shane added. “He’s NOT dead. He’s very much alive and is causing a lot of trouble in Linn County.”

"Then who's in the coffin six feet under?"

Billy came up with a suggestion. "Well, let's just dig it up and find out, okay?"

"Are you kidding me. I like my job. If I touch that particular site, I'll be mowing lawns in Alaska or further north, get my drift, kiddo?"

Marty put his hand on the short guy's shoulder. "Is the situation that serious?"

"You betcha! It's that serious. The irate relatives of Mrs. Snodgrass are still in a legal battle with Central Cemetery to get the guy's coffin out of their family's plot. They need permission to move Ron Thomas' coffin, but his only relative is his brother, Frankie Thomas. Frankie won't give his permission because he claims he and John had converted to Islam, so the body can't be moved, because it would violate the dignity and sanctity of the deceased. There's been a court case hanging in the air for the last five years, still tied up in appeals and pending consideration by the Oregon Supreme Court. If he's alive, they'll be elated to find out and get their grandmother buried correctly."

"Where's her coffin buried?" Shane wanted to know.

"The drunkard put her body where the Ron Thomas headstone is located, so it remains this way even today. We can't do anything until the courts settle the issue. If he's alive, as you say, then we'll eventually be able to solve this mess. What a headache this has been for the cemetery owners."

Billy advised the caretaker, "He's alive all right. Alive and robbing small stores in the area. I wonder if he's going to do something about this problem?"

"What problem?"

"The problem of us knowing he's alive. I think he'll want to come out here and dig up his coffin and dispose of the evidence that he's not actually inside it."

"I hope I'm not here when he comes. He sounds like an unsavory kind of fellow. I don't think I want to make his acquaintance."

Chapter 8
A Grave Situation

The school was abuzz with gossip about the robbery at Centwise. Engelbert Farnsworth III was not well-liked. He could count his friends on one hand, and that included his parents and Spot, his German Shepherd. The consensus was that he deserved anything he got. Some of the Lacombites might have thought the same thing, but they'd never make that idea verbal. Billy made it clear to everyone. "If we said everything we thought, or people could read our minds, we probably wouldn't have a friend left in this world." After wrestling practice, the kids went to the police station.

Marty was the first to enter Sergeant Kochian's office. "We want to know if there's any legal process being started to release Mark Traker from prison in Salem, seeing that Ron Thomas is on the loose and not buried in the coffin at the cemetery?"

"I understand your concern, but these legal maneuvers take time. Besides that, there's no PROOF he's alive, just Shane's word that he saw him in Boise." Sergeant Kochian believed Shane, but that wasn't enough to speed up the legal process.

Erin was right behind her brother. "Then we want to find out who collected the insurance payment. We believe this is just a case of insurance fraud, don't you?"

"If everything you say is correct, it appears to be just that. I looked into the idea, trying to stay ahead of you guys enough to deserve my salary. I found out the beneficiary was a person by the name of John Brown, a resident of Scio."

Billy wasn't impressed. "John Brown, huh! It's a very common name in the United States. I bet Ron Thomas was posing as John Brown. All he'd have to do is make a fake driver's license and try to collect the insurance money. What's the address of this so-called John Brown?"

"He lives at 206 South Main Street in Scio. What're you kids thinking about doing? You know I don't like you putting yourselves into the line of fire."

"We wouldn't do that. Just finding out if someone lives at that address will be sufficient. Did anyone actually collect $100,000 from the unfortunate insurance company?" Erin wanted to know.

The sergeant responded to Erin's concern. "The way I understand it, John Brown didn't have enough personal information to verify he was the actual person on the policy. Therefore, the Mutual of Omaha Insurance Company did NOT pay the claim. That must've made Ron Thomas really mad. I'm sure he felt it necessary to leave the state, which is why you came across him at the Boise airport. It was just a stroke of luck."

"Come on, Sergeant, you go to church," Billy informed him. "You know who we are and what we believe. Luck had nothing to do with it. I'm sure God wants Mark Traker out of jail, and He's using the information we know to do it. It's going to get done. All we need to do is get Ron Thomas behind bars, where he belongs."

"Proving he's alive and getting Traker out of prison still doesn't assure us that Thomas will be caught, tried, and get time behind bars. There are a lot of crooked lawyers just itching to make a name for themselves with a case like this, getting him off, and all."

Billy was thinking again. "Something else bothers me. To pull this off, Thomas had to have some help from someone who declared him dead. Who exactly would do that?"

"That would be a coroner. He probably worked for the state. I'll look up the case and find out who that was, stand by." The sergeant made a few calls and came back with an answer. "The person who declared him dead was working for the state. Her name is Mary Johnson."

"Is this a joke?" Marty wanted to know, smirking.

"What is so funny, kid?"

"It's just too much of a joke. Really! This is also a very common name. Didn't you notice anything funny about the name?" Now, everyone was chuckling.

"That's what they told me, Mary Johnson!"

Shane was still snickering. "The more we look into this case, the stranger it appears. Where's this Johnson lady right now?"

"This is what I don't understand. According to the person I just talked to, this Johnson lady hasn't been seen since the funeral. It appears she just vanished, gone without a trace."

Billy had a smart remark, "I'm surprised they didn't tell you she was beaten to death with a left-handed hammer."

The sergeant wasn't amused. "They said she had a relative in the area by the name of John Smith." Now the Lacombites and Bowie were busting a gut laughing. The poor sergeant was smiling, but he didn't know why. "Okay, that's enough! Now what's so funny?"

Billy smiled at the police officer, "Sir, all these names are on the list of the most common names used in America."

Now the chief was laughing too. He heard some chucking coming from the other side of the room, where his patrolmen were. "Okay, that's it. You guys are too much. I can't take all this comedy in one sitting. I suppose you'll want John's address too?"

"It's probably somewhere in Hollywood, don't you think, Chief?" Shane finished, "where Curly, Larry, and Moe live. We don't have enough gas to go there today, maybe next week, though."

Erin wasn't done yet. "I suppose you don't know anything about the funeral director, whose name is on the burial certificate?"

George Kochian read it off the document. "His name is Robert Green." That was too much for the Lacomb crew.

As they were getting into the Chevy to leave, Billy made another comment after he stopped laughing. "There's something weird about all of this. No one caught on to the use of the most common names in the United States? They just let things ride as they were? Man, someone was asleep at the wheel when this ridiculous caper went down." The group drove to Scio.

Arriving at the address the Sergeant had written down, led the five of them to an empty lot. Marty was the first to notice. "Well, well, well, what a surprise! The address takes us to an empty lot. Unless John Brown is a field mouse, he doesn't live here, now does he?"

The 13-mile ride back to Lacomb was uneventful. The vote was unanimous to go to the cemetery and dig up the grave of Ron Thomas in the plot of Olga to prove there was no body in that coffin. The next day, they discovered someone else had beaten them to it.

The *Lebanon Express* reported that someone had violated sacred ground. A plot marked Ron Thomas was dug up, and the hoodlum left the open coffin displaying the remains of a lady. They were positive it was Olga McIntosh Snodgrass. Why she was buried in Ron Thomas' place was yet to be discovered.

Bowie was smiling. "Ron Thomas dug up the wrong coffin? Wow, he must've been petrified when he opened the box and found a real body in there."

"He's a desperate man," the spindle-legged wrestler replied. "He's without friends and broke. That's why he robbed the Centwise Drug Store."

There was a meeting of the Linn County Junior Detectives at the T.P. Oil Company. Shane wanted everyone to be included in the excitement and the work!

Nobody in their right mind would be found dead digging around in a cemetery, especially after dark. But whoever said these kids were in their right minds? "Black as midnight, and cold as the inside of a beggar's tomb" was the description Marty gave the evening, as they took off from the gas station with shovels and picks in the trunk.

A few ghost stories were told before they arrived. Shane wanted all of them to be in the mood. "Shane, if you tell one more story," Bowie threatened, "you'll have to do all the work yourself, dig?"

The cemetery was dark as the inside of a cow. "Lonely" was the description Kosette gave it. Nothing stirred, nothing even whispered a sound. The temperature had dropped to 30 degrees. The sky was totally overcast. Fog was moving above the headstones.

Kosy stuttered. "I ... I think my Grandma is calling me. See you guys later, okay?"

Bowie was hesitant. "I've been to places I detested that were better than this."

Erin was mumbling. "I'd have the weebie geebies if I were here at high noon."

Billy gulped hard. “Right now, my heart’s in my throat, and my stomach went south for the winter. I can feel the dampness and the deadness.”

Marty, being the oldest, was a bit more reserved. “There’s nothing to be afraid of, everyone has to die sometime, right guys?”

Shane was shocked at his companions’ concerns. “Come on, you scaredy cats. There’s nothing here but a bunch of dead people, who can’t hurt you.”

“It’s not the dead people I’m worried about,” the Nez Perce shuddered. “How’s one very alive Ron Thomas, for instance?

With the flashlight, they began hunting for the headstone of poor Olga McIntosh Snodgrass. There was no one to hinder their search, but two investigating eyes were following their every move.

Chapter 9
The Empty Tomb

Billy was stationed on a marble monument and told to keep his ears open for strange sounds.

The digging began with a solid crunch of a pick ax. This wasn't the most desirable job to have. None of the kids had any experience in such low-down work. "This job gives me the creeps, and I'm not kidding," and Marty WASN'T kidding.

Erin tried to lighten the mood. "Did you know Bowie, that a rut is just a grave with the ends kicked out. Be positive, optimistic, and you'll be just like the mortician golfer, he was always up on the last hole."

Digging a hole six by three by seven would not usually break a sweat in 30-degree weather. But when that hole happens to be in the middle of a midnight cemetery and the bottom of the hole has a coffin, there are other reasons a person might perspire—like fear, nervousness, or cowardice. Take your pick.

Bowie wanted to change the tone of the evening. "If anyone was ever caught messing around in old Native American burial grounds, he was punished severely. I don't suppose you white men take any lighter look at the crime, do you?"

"I can't remember," Marty said as he scratched his head. "The last time I was caught grave robbing, I was under ten years old, still a child. Therefore, I didn't have to do anything except work my way through reform school, selling *Hotrod* magazines door to door."

The work was exhausting, so the grave diggers had to switch off every ten minutes. The girls were cheering them on with encouraging phrases like: "Hurry up, I'm freezing," "Can't you dig any quieter," and "Let's hope we've got the right one."

The dirt was stacking high enough to fall back down into the hole. It was Bowie's turn in the pit. "Hey, you guys, try to pull some of the dirt off to the side. I'm being buried alive in here, and that's not what I had in mind when I signed up with this chicken outfit."

Erin started pushing the dirt aside with her hands.

Billy yelled at the whole crew. "There's a car coming down the road."

Bowie bounded out of the grave and called everyone

together for a pow-wow. Marty came up with the best idea. "Shine the light on him like we're supposed to be here. If it's Ron Thomas, he'll drive on by. He doesn't want to be caught out here."

A nearby owl gave its opinion of the whole clandestine operation by asking a simple question, "WHOOOO?" Kosy was just a bystander, so she answered the nocturnal hunter. "Ron Thomas, that's WHOOOO, my little feathered friend, who else?"

The car stopped and the driver shut off the motor. He opened the door and headed for the trunk. Before he could open it, he was hit with three powerful flashlights. He pulled his coat collar up over his face and rushed back to the front door, starting the engine even before he had his door closed.

The panicky driver revved the motor and tore out of the parking lot like he'd seen a ghost, or like he had sat on some fire ants. There wasn't anything left of him except two taillights.

With that reaction, the kids became even more nervous. "I'm presuming the driver was the man who's supposed to be buried in this hole, or some kid looking for fun, do you suppose?" Billy suggested.

Kosy volunteered weakly, "I vote on the second idea, how about you, Erin?"

The mysterious car left the graveyard and turned toward Albany. The kids resumed work, with Marty in the hole. Thirty minutes later, with Shane digging, there was a repeated thudding noise as the shovel hit something.

"I think we've struck gold," Billy reported from his hear-out perch. "That could only be the coffin making that hollow noise, right, gang?"

Marty jumped into the hole and helped Shane clear off the final inches of dirt. They were standing on top of a wooden casket.

Marty looked faint, "Be still, my heart, lest I go deaf from the noise, or is it Shane's knees getting to know one another that's sounding off?"

They tipped the coffin up on its end, and with the help of the unwilling girls, they hoisted it out and laid it on the ground. Erin was bemoaning the fact that she got her hands dirty, and Kosy didn't like the idea of breaking a fingernail.

"Girls, girls," Bowie scowled, "it's a very important moment in Linn County history, and they have to be concerned about their looks."

Shane defended their femininity. "Come on, Bowie, that's what we like about them, right, Marty?"

Marty was sitting on top of the coffin, and Billy was dying to know what was happening. "Come on, you guys, quit leaving me in the dark. What's going on? Did you open it yet?"

Bowie wasn't inclined to volunteer. "It's been five years since the burial, plenty of time for decomposing, even if he wasn't a dead musician, right, Billy?"

"Right, big guy, now who's going to open the coffin?"

No one jumped up to answer the call to duty. Finally, there was a shuffling of dead leaves and some movement behind the trees to the left of the grave diggers. Everyone froze in their tracks and pointed their flashlights in that direction.

A bright flashlight broke the darkness, and a booming voice sliced through the icy night air. "Don't anyone move. You're all under arrest."

Nobody wanted to be under arrest, especially six do-gooders who are trying to help a condemned man prove his innocence. But that's what the officer said, "I said, you're all under arrest for violating this sacred place."

There were six jaws to be retrieved from the ground, as the kids could hardly believe their bad luck. Officer Freeburg stepped out into the open and identified himself. "I can't believe my eyes. You kids have been doing all this vandalism out here in the cemetery?"

They were all relieved to discover the voice that had stopped all their hearts belonged to a friend—Officer Quinten Freeburg of the Lebanon Police Department. At least they weren't in as much trouble as some of them had imagined.

Shane was the first to defend their actions. "I know it does seem rather strange, us being here with these picks and shovels in our hands, beside this apparent open grave, doesn't it?"

"Keep talking, Shane," the officer encouraged. "Maybe you will even convince me not to put handcuffs on the lot of you. What in the world are you doing, anyway? The explanation had better be without any lies, please."

Marty replaced Shane as the spokesman. "We really haven't broken any laws, officer. For you see, there's no body in that coffin. We've been unfortunate enough to have seen Ron Thomas twice, and Billy heard him three times. This is his grave site, and we're looking at his coffin, but it's empty."

The officer was confused and didn't mind saying so. "What are you trying to say? Come on, spit it out, without stuttering, please."

Officer Quinten Freeburg was filled in on the whole story, from the very beginning–the airport in Boise, Idaho. He listened quite intently and nodded now and then. He liked these kids and wasn't too excited about any formal charges against them.

"I guess the proof of the pudding is in the eating, as they say. We'll have to open the coffin to see what's really under the lid, now won't we?"

Marty was ready for someone to do it, but there was still no volunteer. "Maybe the good officer would do us a kind act and open the lid? What do you say, gang, should we leave the pleasure to him?"

The vote was unanimous. The officer didn't know if he was being honored or shanghaied. "OK, you guys, I'll do it for you, and this should decide: you'll either be heroes or delinquents."

They leaned the coffin against a tree and the officer struggled to open it. "Give me that pick ax. If this isn't on the level, you kids will have to buy a new casket, understood?"

Billy was trying to make light of the whole thing to take all the stress off. "First, Officer, I think you should know the average body contains enough bones to make an entire skeleton. With this, I rest my case."

After digesting all this nerdy humor, six teens nodded, glad to have the officer do the unveiling. With just a little more prying, the lid broke free. The officer opened the top and slammed it shut with an ashen face.

He looked at the kids with regret in his eyes. "You kids are in BIG trouble. There's a skeleton in here!"

Chapter 10
Meeting the Governor

Billy moved around restlessly, and Bowie started to sweat profusely. Erin and Kosy began wringing their hands, and Marty gulped hard. Shane was the only one who didn't seem nervous. He shook his head, disputing the officer's conclusions but not his vision.

"That can't be possible, Officer Freeburg. It just can't be possible." Shane walked over to the coffin and opened the lid to see for himself. He stared in at the contents and closed the lid slowly.

"There's something fishy here. If that were a real skeleton in there, the casket would be filled with more than just bones and rocks. Right?" Then Shane began to laugh. It seemed inappropriate.

Officer Freeburg didn't understand what was going on, so how could he appreciate it?

Shane kept laughing until Bowie stepped over and put his hand on his mouth. "Why don't you fill us in on your comedy act, Shane? I'm sure the good officer would like to know what's so funny, right?"

"Well, there's a skeleton in here all right, but it's the one that was stolen from the biology class at school. Remember the break-in and the furor that followed?

The school had just received it, and someone stole it. That was five years ago. I've heard so much about it because there have been a lot of jokes going around.

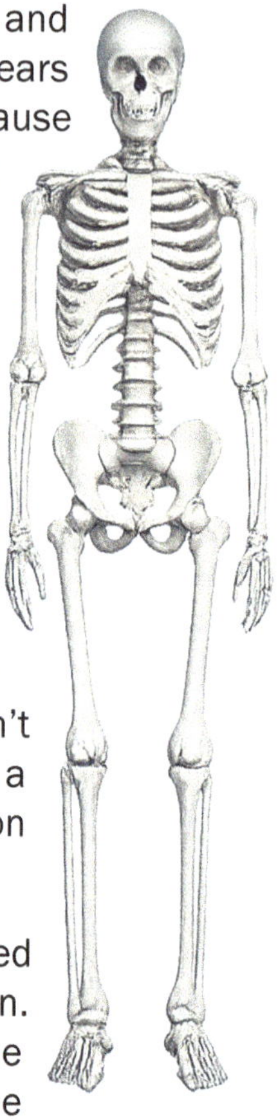

"Jokes like, the only one graduating this year has already left the school. And even a bony person can't stand the rigors of biology class."

Marty was the only sophomore in the group. "I remember. They called him 'Freddie the Freeloader.' One joke was about him joining the wrestling team because he wouldn't have to lose weight. Another one was a comment that he was the only one on campus with a backbone."

The officer looked again and fumbled around with the contents of the coffin. There was no doubt about it. Shane was right on the mark. It was the one from LUHS. It even said so on the back of the skull—*"Donated to LUHS by Dr. and Mrs. Nadine Girod December 13, 1957."*

"He's a doctor in a clinic on Park Street. His wife is Nadine Girod, and she's a close friend of my mother's," Billy informed them.

"I misjudged you kids. I should've known better. Sergeant Kochian has the highest regard for all of you. It seems he's very thankful that, unlike some of the teens at LUHS, your group actually makes his job easier, especially during Halloween and New Year's

Eve.

"He's always saying good things about your expertise in finding trouble and using your #1 detective, Billy Evans, to solve a lot of problems for you. Now, what can we conclude from this empty coffin?"

Billy didn't want to disappoint the good lawman, so he started sharing some of his deductions. "Well, for starters,

1) Shane was right when he said Ron Thomas was working in Boise, Idaho,

2) Mark Traker has served five years for a crime he didn't commit,

3) There has to have been someone else involved to collect the insurance, and

4) There has been a crime committed, and it was insurance fraud."

Officer Freeburg liked Billy's analyses. "It looks like you, Billy, have read a lot of Sherlock Holmes, or listened to a multitude of Perry Mason's court cases on TV.

This is serious stuff. If Ron Thomas finds out you're messing in his life like this, it could be dangerous for you."

The California transplant reassured the officer of their intentions. "We've no plans to confront anyone. We have a friend in State Prison who's innocent, and we need to get this new information to Sergeant Kochian ASAP. Can you help us?"

"You betcha I can. I'm glad to get an innocent man out of prison. I'll call him right now. Stand by." With that promise, the good patrolman went to his car and began explaining the whole situation to Sergeant Kochian. The chief of police wanted to talk to Shane.

"Shane, what in the world are you doing digging up graves. It's against the law, you know."

"Well, friend, we knew that but were willing to take a chance that this coffin was empty. AND IT IS EMPTY! Now we know Ron Thomas is not dead, and we can start the legal process to get our friend Mark Traker out of State Prison, right?"

"You kids were taking a real risk. What if he'd been in the area?"

"It was a risk we were willing to take to help our friend in State Prison Sergeant," Shane said.

"I understand, but I still don't like you kids getting into harm's way. Now get down here to the station."

Shane assured him they were on the way. Upon arriving at the headquarters, they noticed the patrolmen sitting in a circle, laughing their heads off. Billy followed the frolics and stopped tapping his white cane right in front of them. "Hey, friends, what's so knee-slapping funny?"

The new officer, Gabriel Thomas Sosa, explained it. "We keep a record of the Oregon Stupid Club, and someone in Coos Bay, Oregon, just joined it."

"What is the Oregon Stupid Club?" Kosy asked.

"It's an involuntary club you automatically join if you demonstrate that you're dumber than dirt while committing a crime."

"So, who just joined the club and why?" Billy wanted to know.

"There's this guy, Lee Bare, a kid from Mobile, Alabama. He went into a bank in Coos Bay and wrote a note to the teller demanding she give him all the money in her till. She did, and he took off with the loot. As soon as he got home, the police surrounded his place and arrested him."

"So, what is so funny about that?" Billy asked.

Officer Gabriel could hardly tell Billy because he was

laughing so hard. "He wrote the note on the back of a deposit slip from his OWN checkbook. It had his name and address right on the piece of paper. Now, should he join the club or not?"

"Only if you put him on the page of the dumbest ones! Maybe you should consider that." The Jewish kid suggested.

"Good idea, Billy," Officer Gabriel concurred.

Billy scooted over to the chief's desk. "So what're we going to do to get our friend out of State Prison, Chief?"

With the phone still up to his ear, Sergeant Kochian turned to the kids. "I have Governor Carol Baye on the line. She wants to know if you kids have junior detective badges; if not, she wants me to issue all of you one.

"This case has bothered her for the last three years. She said every week she gets a letter from Mark Traker insisting that he's innocent, and now you've proven he really is. She wants you to be in her office tomorrow after school. Can you go up to Salem?"

Bowie made a suggestion. "Ask her if it can be after wrestling practice?"

The sergeant chatted with the governor for a few minutes. "She said to be in her office at 8:00 PM, on the mark. Can you make it?"

Erin piped in, "We can, and we will. Tell her we appreciate it."

Kosy also wanted to go. "We'll have to take two cars because I'm not going to stand watch at a graveyard and not see the governor. I'll have someone drive me to the school, and I'll meet you there at 5:30 PM. Is that okay with all of you?"

They all agreed. Erin was ecstatic. "Wow, I'll have time to take a shower and do my hair after cheerleading practice."

The parents and grandparents were surprised but pleased to let them go on their own. Grandma Julia wanted them to take a few jars of canned peaches to the governor. "Tell her I voted for her."

The cars pulled out of the LUHS parking lot at 5:30 on the nose. It took them two hours to reach the domed Capitol building. They were able to admire some of the fabulous paintings inside the building before the governor called them into her office.

"Well, what have we here? Sergeant Kochian informed me that you guys have helped him a lot in the last five months. Who's the brains of this outfit? He told me it was the kid with the white cane. Is that right?"

Billy had been in the back. When he heard her mention him, he moved to the front as the troop opened a hole for him to pass. “That would be me, Your Honorable Governor. Billy Evans at your service!”

“Have a seat, Billy. The policeman also told me all of you boys wrestle for Jim Hazewinkel. I knew him when we studied together at Oregon State. That was a few years ago, of course. Is he a good coach?”

“He certainly is. What is it about Mark Traker’s case that got you so interested and involved, if you don’t mind me asking?”

“Not at all, Billy. It was the constant letters insisting he was innocent.”

Bowie piped in. “But, Governor, you must get a lot of those letters, right?“

”Huh, big, wide, and brown-skinned. You must be Bowie Pinetree, the Nez Perce from Pendleton, right?”

“Wow, the Governor really does her homework, now doesn’t she?” Bowie said.

“That’s what the fine people of Oregon pay me for,

now don't they?" The LUHS Warriors saw her sneak in a warm smile when she made this last statement. She was obviously a well-trained politician. "It was the sincerity of his letters and the strange circumstances of the case. What caught my eye in the case was the phony guy who tried to collect the insurance money.

"They denied John Brown's claim because he couldn't produce enough personal information to confirm his identity. Then he disappears from the face of the earth, and no one ever hears from him again. That was too unbelievable to be true. And then there were all those common names on the documents. The teenagers liked this woman; she seemed to be up on all the right stuff.

"But, all in all, I didn't have enough evidence to set Mark free. Now you kids have come up with the facts we all missed. Wow, how we need more teenagers like you guys, making our work easier instead of harder.

"I have the power to pardon Mark Traker, not exonerate him. But a pardon is good enough for now. I called you here because I wanted you to be present when I go to the prison and get him out of there. So, you kids follow me. Can you do that?"

So, again, here they were, following a police car with its light and siren blasting away. It was an exciting ride to the State Prison. Mark had been advised and was ready to check out. They gave him the belongings he had left at the front gate when he entered there five years ago. They included: one red Swiss Army knife, one pack of Lucky Strike cigarettes, a Zippo Lighter, three Bazooka bubble gums, five seashells, and $2.47 in change. Mark told them to keep the smokes; he had permanently quit a long time ago.

When he came through the gate, he saw Shane, and his face lit up with a smile as wide as the Montana horizon. He just shook his head and hugged the grappler.

With tears in his eyes, he stammered, "I ... I ... don't have the proper words to express the feelings in my heart. But for now, THANKS A MILLION, might do. I'm not sure what to do now. I don't even have enough money for a bus ride to nowhere, which is exactly where I'm headed, because I don't have anywhere to go."

Kosy was teary-eyed too. "We've already talked to our family, and you can stay with us until you find a job and can rent a place of your own. We know you, and you're our friend."

The governor was trying to hold back the tears, but

wasn't doing a very good job. "I'm so glad you finally were proven innocent, Mark. I'm dreadfully sorry for the last five years. I'm going to try to get some monetary help for you to make up for these wasted years.

"As far as you kids go, I believe you have a wrestling meet here in South Salem on the 12th. I plan to be there. I can't promise I'll be rooting for you because my own children attend there. But, I'll be at the meet anyway."

Billy wanted more information. "Why are you so taken up with wrestling? Our sport doesn't generate enough interest to make it in most newspapers. We usually get about as much press coverage as the Kiwanis Ladies Badminton Team."

"Well, for your information, my cousin, Terry McCann, was on the 1960 Olympic Freestyle Team that went to Rome. He won a gold medal. Our family has been avid fans ever since. I admire the tenacity and hard work that wrestlers have to go through to be successful. God bless all of you for what you've done for Mark."

The kids had to stop at the T&R truck plaza for a hamburger before turning east toward Lebanon, then Lacomb, for the rest of the trip. Mark sat in the front next to Erin. "Man, five years wasted. I wonder what I'll do now. I have no family. Do you really think I can get a job?"

"Grandpa has already found you one at Snow Peak Logging Company, if you want to work there. They need another choke setter, starting Monday. Is that okay with you?"

Everyone seemed happy, content that their friend, who had been unjustly locked up for many years, had been released. BUT, not everyone was elated. There was a certain grave robber and store robber who was not at all content. He had kept up with the proceedings and knew exactly what had just happened.

Chapter 11
Released from Sin's Penalty

The wrestling practice was intense because there was a meet on the 12th against an old, powerful rival—South Salem. The capital schools were always bigger and therefore could muster a better team. Their coach, Rudenei Silva Costa, was the South American champion from Brazil. It was a small sport there, but seemed to be growing. Rude's assistant, Ronnie Simmons, was from Oklahoma State and had won several national titles as a high school student, although he didn't win any in college.

These two knew Jim Hazewinkel and always gave him a bad time when the schools met. It was all in fun, but Jim thought it would be MORE fun if he actually beat them once. He was in his prime at Monday's practice.

"Listen up, you wimps. South Salem is a real team, not like the ones we've seen around here. They're so tough they use thumbtacks to hold up their socks and manhole covers for frisbees." They knew this was a thought so old it was already collecting social security, but they didn't want to hurt the Coach's feelings, so they said nothing about it.

Doug Hazewinkel, Jim's brother, whispered to Shane, "He says that every year—the same line. The problem is, it's absolutely true. They have a really tough team, and it'll take all of our expertise to beat them. I think we can do it if we put our weakest grappler against their best one."

After practice, Bowie's Nash went straight to the T.P. Oil Company. Shane had been leaving his '57 Chevy there because of so much vandalism against the classic car. "No sense in taking any chances. This car draws a lot of attention."

Mark Traker lived in a small shed on the Woods farm.

It only had a bed and a closet. He had to eat with the family and use the outside plumbing behind his shed. He was allowed to take a shower twice a week, on Wednesday and Saturday. Jack had known Mark for years, so they hit it off.

The work of a choke setter at Snow Peak Lumber Company was a difficult change from the routine of prison life. Mark had gotten a little used to a simple schedule and light work. The only work he did at the State Prison was to make license plates for five hours a day. Besides that, it was eat, sleep, and read books or watch movies. However, he did manage to make it to the gym and lift weights. He was very muscular.

His chokesetter job consisted of attaching the cable with a knob and fitting ball to logs that were down in ravines. After the cable is locked on, the caterpillar pulls the log up the side of the hill. It's the most dangerous job in the lumber industry and is usually given to the newest man. The new men say a choker's job is an instrument of torture invented by people who hate loggers.

His job was hard, sweaty, and very dangerous. Grandma Julia packed him a great lunch. It was usually a ham sandwich with tomatoes, lettuce, bacon, and pickles, followed by a slice of her famous nothing chocolate cake, washed down with a thermos of hot coffee. This meal was something to look forward to.

Mark Traker had a difficult background. His parents separated when he was just two years old. The father disappeared and was never heard from again. Lida, his mother, tried working as a waitress at a small cafe in Jefferson, Oregon. They lived in a two-room shed with the plumbing outside. It wasn't nice, but it was better than it would've been in International Falls, Minnesota, where she was raised. That place was just 30 miles from the Canadian border, where the temperatures can hit -70° in January, if the wind is howling.

When he went to school, the other kids would tease him for his ragged clothes and shoes with holes in the soles. He put cardboard in the shoes to keep out the cold. If they got wet, he had to change the cardboard. His lunch consisted of one slice of bread with butter on it and a crabapple he picked from a neighbor's tree along the road to school.

His mother made enough money to pay the rent and keep the wolf away. Lida depended heavily on welfare and on some kind people at the Faith Baptist church in Lebanon. She never attended services, but some members thought there was always hope she would.

In high school, there was too much embarrassment, so Mark quit. He got a job at the Lebanon Community Center. He called himself a Flat Surface Engineer, but he really was just a janitor. Working there for 10 years, he managed to get by. He looked like a nice guy, and that's how Ron Thomas picked him out as a patsy to be set up for the insurance fraud.

Now he was out and hoping never to see the bum again. It cost him five years at State Prison, five long years he could never get back. All he wanted to do was to earn some honest money and get on with his life. Both Jack and Julia were witnessing to Mark. He knew their lifestyles before they were Christians. "I didn't know you two were religious people, NOW you are?"

Julia wanted to clarify the subject. “Religious, we never were, and still aren’t religious people.”

“How is that? You go to church every Sunday and Wednesday, read the Bible all the time, pray before you eat, and don’t cuss, smoke, or drink. In my book, that makes you a religious person.”

“Mark, religion comes in many packages, a multitude of forms. Religion is man’s attempt to impress his deity and win his favor, allowing a pleasant afterlife. These people think good works are the way to win this favor. Some think they do, others believe they fall short of the mark, and the rest give up trying. Usually, a religious leader will encourage his followers to obey their set of rules to obtain eternal bliss.”

“That sounds about right. I think that’s logical, don’t you?”

“The problem, my friend, is that Jehovah, the only God, is holy and no sin will go unpunished. Another problem is that we’re sinners who can’t do anything to settle the condemnation we must face at the judgment seat.”

“Julia, I don’t understand. You mean all the good I do doesn’t count one iota with God? If that is true, how do you explain His insistence that we keep the Ten Commandments?”

“The Ten Commandments are a good moral code, but God never promised that one could be saved by keeping them. Besides that, do you know ANYONE who has kept even these ten? The Bible says we’ve all lied and sinned. Romans 3:10 says, ‘For all have sinned and come short of the glory of God.’ The Ten Commandments don’t mention how we resolve our sin problem with God, do they? How will humanity resolve this sin problem?"

Mark replied. "I don't know. I only need to take care of myself, I suppose. I know I haven't kept them, far from it. What I want to know is, if good works can't save me, which I always thought they could, then what do I need to be saved?"

"If good works could save anyone, then Christ died in vain. The Bible says this. We know He didn't die in vain. Do you know the story of the two thieves who died, one on each side of Christ?"

"Yes, I do. One rejected Christ. The other acknowledged Him, and Christ said to that thief, 'Today you shall be with me in Paradise.' Did I quote it correctly?"

"Yeah, you did! It is a famous story. What did the thief who went to Paradise do? Did he attend a church, get baptized, give money, or help the poor? What was it he did to be translated to Paradise with Christ when he died?"

"He believed in Him."

"That's right. And that's exactly what Jesus explained in all of his teachings to the common people, religious leaders, and to His Apostles."

"But I've always believed Christ was the Savior. Then I'm saved, right? I'll go to heaven, right?"

"Let me give you an example. Look at this chair. Does it look like a good sturdy chair? Strong enough to do the job?"

"Yes."

"Is it holding you up?"

"Nope, not yet."

"You're practicing what's called 'mental consent.' You believe with your mind."

"Isn't that enough?"

"Do you believe this chair can support your weight? Do you believe it is trustworthy enough to sit down on?"

"Yes, I do."

"What do you have to do for it to hold you up?"

"I have to sit down on it, put my whole weight on it, depend on it, and trust it."

"That's the difference. You believe Christ is the Savior, but you've never sat down, never trusted Him, never put your weight of sin on Him. Therefore, you're not saved. Are you understanding what I'm trying to explain here? Mental consent concerning Christ isn't enough; it won't open the Pearly Gates for you. You ARE a religious person, but not a born-again child of God. If you want to spend eternity in heaven, you have to do what Christ clearly explained by saying that we 'MUST' be born again. You have to sit down in the chair."

"What should I do, Julia?"

"You need to confess you're a sinner and accept His sacrifice in your place, you need to receive Him as your Savior, ask Him to save you, and come into your heart. This is what the Bible teaches. It's called being 'born again' and is explained in John chapter three."

"I've never had it explained to me quite like that. It seems clear to me, then, what I must do. Will you pray with me? I'm not too good at it. I haven't prayed for many years. The last time I prayed, I was saying the now-I-lay-me-down-to-sleep type prayers."

"I'd be glad to help you, Mark. But prayer is just talking to God, telling Him how you feel and what you want.

You go first. If you stumble and need help, pause, and I'll help you."

The man who spent five years in State Prison, who was framed and wasted all that time, knelt on the floor in Julia Woods' kitchen.

> Lord, I'm not very good at this. I've believed that Jesus was the Savior, but as Julia said, I've never sat down in the chair of faith and trusted Him to save me. I know I've sinned, and I understand now that good works won't resolve this problem between us.
>
> Lord, I spent five years in prison for something I didn't do. You knew I was innocent and sent Shane to prove it. Thank you for this grace. I repent of my sin and ask You, Jesus, the Son of God, to come into my heart and save me today. I believe and want to spend eternity with You and these wonderful friends. I want the Pearly Gates to open for me when I leave this life. Thank You, Lord, for hearing me and saving me. Amen

The trees were bare in Linn County, except for the evergreens. The January weather was cold and wet. Hunting season was over months ago, and people were cutting Douglas fir trees to keep in stock with winter fuel. Most Oregonians were getting ready for Valentine's Day. But, during all this busy activity in Oregon, there was rejoicing in the presence of the angels of God for one sinner, Mark Traker, who put his trust in Jesus. Because he was born again, he'll find his name in the book of life, allowing him to spend eternity with Jesus and all the saints. This was a glorious winter day in the Willamette Valley!

Julia was so thrilled to have this opportunity to lead Mark to Christ. She had so many household responsibilities that she rarely got across Crabtree Creek. Usually, it was only to do some grocery shopping on Saturday and attend church on Sundays and Wednesdays.

God brought this man to her house so she could explain salvation to him, and she did explain it in a very simple manner. Mark understood it perfectly and was made a child of God, eternally saved. When the kids got home and heard the news, they ran straight for Mark's one-room shed. He was sitting on his Army fold-away cot reading the Bible. He greeted them warmly.

The new believer was smiling and ready to tell his story. He didn't leave out any of the details. He even included the good illustration using the chair. The kid's happiness for his salvation was only exceeded by his own joy in knowing he'd spend eternity with them and with Christ.

Chapter 12
Logging Accident

The wrestling meet with South Salem turned out just as it was hyped up to be—close and tough. The Warriors took the lead with Billy's 5-2 win. Then they lost it when Bob Bardwell was pinned. Shane won by two points, Bert was pinned, Dennis Hinds won by one point, returning the lead to the Warriors. Marty pinned his opponent. Dave Carlson won in overtime.

Governor Carol Baye was there and actually stood up and cheered for Shane. When she realized her mistake, she started scratching her back like she had the hives, trying to redeem herself in front of the South Salem crowd. The Warriors knew what was going on and threw lots of smiles her way.

As usual, the outcome depended on Bowie. He didn't like it, but that was life, as he always said. He started badly. The Nez Perce was taken down, giving his opponent two points. Bowie tied it with a reversal in the final period, and the match went into overtime. With a leg sweep, the Nez Perce got two points and won his match, winning the meet 28-27.

Jim Hazewinkel went into the stands to greet the governor, shaking her hand and wishing her well. She leaned over and whispered, "I hope you win a lot of meets this year. I'll be expecting to see some state champions in March, in Portland. See you then."

Mark Traker was able to see the meet. He was thrilled to see his friends with their arms held up in victory. His life as a teenager wasn't so wonderful. That's why he was extremely pleased to be part of these lives he had begun to love dearly. These are the junior detectives who earned his pardon, getting him out of State Prison.

Coach Hazewinkel was very pleased but didn't let his guard down; he never did. "Listen up, you wimps, this victory was well-deserved. You did exactly what I told you to do, and now we have only a few weaker teams left before the regionals and state championship. I believe we can win the state title if we don't let up. We need more sweat and more repetitions. We can do it."

January in Linn County is cold, rainy, and very humid. If someone wants to ski, they have to drive to Hoodo or Mount Hood, since Snow Peak is not accessible. The peak seems harmless enough, but it has claimed more than its share of lives from careless hikers to lost campers. Snowstorms will hit the mountain without fair warning. Some unfortunate outdoors people have never been found.

Around the Lebanon/Lacomb area, there's very little snow. Most Lebanonese prefer it that way. As Bowie always says, "Who wants to shovel the white manure, anyway? Snow does make more money for our gas station, though. People get stuck, and we have to dig them out. Their car batteries fail, and we get paid to jump-start them."

Ron Thomas was still in hiding, hoping for a chance to eke out some revenge on the goody-two-shoes who had dug up his coffin and proved he wasn't in it. He had spent some time robbing small stores around Linn County, making enough to keep the wolf way from his front door.

His time in Boise, Idaho, wasn't a success. The rotten teenagers spotted him at the airport cafeteria, and he had to zoom out of there. His rusted-out Willys was on its last leg. It was blowing out more black smoke than a diesel logging truck loaded down with Douglas fir trees. He had to change stolen cars every week to keep ahead of the law.

He had to find a way to keep out of jail and still get his revenge. It was the only thing that occupied his mind, day and night. He hated the thought of being outsmarted by some fanatical kids who were still wet behind their ears and didn't know the difference between a polecat and skunk weed.

When he pulled into Sweet Home, he cased the bank, looking for a weakness. Noticing the money truck parked outside was a windfall for him.

If he could distract the guards enough, maybe he could jump into the back and get a few bags of money. It was worth a try. He took off one of his dirty socks and soaked it in gasoline.

Then he pried off a car's gas cap. Stuffing the sock in the gas tank, he lit it with his Zippo lighter. When the car blew sky-high, it distracted the guards. It was like the 4th of July fireworks at the Timber Carnival in Albany.

The heavy, burly guard, Monty Nelson, was standing outside holding a shotgun. He turned to see what was going on. He disobeyed the strict rules when he advanced five steps forward and took his eyes off the open door. The would-be robber jumped into the back of the truck and grabbed two bags full of money. Just as he was about to jump down, the guard slammed the door shut.

"That's it, Bunky, all of the cash is already inside. I locked the door. We can go back to headquarters now. Man, what in the world would make a car blow up like that? I hope they have good insurance."

The ride to the headquarters was quite an experience for Ron Thomas. He had to make some quick decisions, or he was toast for sure. Five blocks from the headquarters, he decided to make his move. He still had his Zippo lighter. Grabbing a handkerchief from his pocket, he lit it, holding it up to the vent on the passenger side of the truck. Smoke started coming out of the truck. "This should do the trick," he thought to himself. He hoped they caught on soon, or he'd be smoked turkey.

The guard, Bill Vaughn, noticed it first. "Hey, Bud, there's smoke coming out of the side of the truck. STOP!"

One guard was standing right behind the other when the door was unlocked. Suddenly, it burst open, pushing them together. Their heads hit, and they were knocked out cold. John hit the ground running, with a money sack in each hand.

He zoomed out of there, thinking he'd hit it big time and could now forget revenge. He already had visions of sitting on a sandy beach in the Caribbean, sipping lemonade and watching the waves beat on the shore.

He found his car and headed north, towards Portland. When he arrived at a private place out of town, he pulled over to take a look at his future. Opening the bags, he discovered something that made his blood boil. Why in the world were they transporting fake money?

Wrestling practice was intense because it was only two weeks until the regionals and, one week later, the state tournament. Shane picked up Kosette at the Green Mountain School building and parked his car at Rocking L Ranch. He took the Jeep to park by the swinging bridge. This was for security reasons.

Arriving at the farmhouse, the two found Julia sitting at the kitchen table with her hands supporting her face. She was weeping bitterly. They had never seen her do this. Something was terribly wrong.

Kosy put her hand on Grandma's shoulder. "What's wrong?"

Julia could hardly stop crying long enough to explain. There ... there was an accident at the logging site today. A cable broke, and the log came rolling back down the ravine. The log killed Mark Traker. He's gone." Shane and Kosy both sat down, dumbfounded, unable to speak.

A choke-setter has the most dangerous job in the lumber industry.

Finally, tears welled up in Kosette's tender eyes. "This is so hard to believe. I just said 'I love you' to him this morning as he walked away, with Grandpa. I don't know what to say." Now she was crying as hard as Julia had been.

Shane was too stunned even to cry or speak. All the work to get Mark out of prison! It wasn't in vain, he told himself. "I'll have to call the others."

Grandma went to the phone. "First, let me call the governor; she'll want to know."

The funeral was scheduled for the following Saturday, at Lacomb Baptist Church. Pastor Ballentine was officiating. He introduced the governor to his congregation. "We're honored to have Governor Carol Baye with us today. She was a great help in securing Mark's pardon. We appreciate your presence, Your

Honorable Governor."

Because of the nature of the accident, there was a closed-casket ceremony. The pastor asked Shane to say a few words before he brought the message.

Shane, dressed in a nice blue suit, strode up to the pulpit. It took him a few minutes to control his emotions. "I am glad the governor is here. Without her help, we couldn't have gotten a pardon for Mark. He spent five years knowing he was innocent and two weeks living free again.

"His body's in this box, but his soul is with our Savior. Mark had been what he described as a semi-religious man. He meant to say that he always believed Christ was the Savior, but had never sat down in the chair. If you want a better explanation of 'the chair,' you can talk to my Grandmother, Julia.

"We knew Mark Traker long before he went to prison. I used to see him now and then, around town. He didn't have a good upbringing, like some of us. When he started living on the farm, he participated in all of our family activities, including meals and family devotions.

"It wasn't long before he started asking questions; good questions. We always answered them with Bible verses or the very words of Jesus Himself. About a week ago, he accepted Christ as his only and sufficient Savior. He's now in the presence of Christ and all the angels of God. He finally has all the answers to the difficult questions we still struggle with.

"I can imagine him sitting down right now, watching a film of creation or the crossing of the Red Sea. I figure God must have it on film so we can all see it. I am looking forward to seeing Daniel in the lion's den and his three friends from the fiery furnace. I envy Mark and will look forward to meeting him there, beside the throne of God, abiding forever."

With these words barely coming out of his mouth, Shane finally finished by saying, "Mark's greatest desire would be to know that someone else trusted Christ as their Savior because of his short witness here. If anyone wants to talk to our pastor about being saved, please see him afterward."

The governor was seen chatting with Pastor Ballentine after the burial at the Lebanon cemetery.

Billy noted something strange. "Here's where it all began, right here at Central Cemetery. It was here that we found out Mark was innocent, although he had known it all along. Ron Thomas is still out there. He's out and about, but not for long. He thinks he's free, but in fact, he's condemned eternally if he doesn't repent and be saved. MARK IS FREE, FOREVER."

TO BE CONTINUED

AUTHOR NOTE: *I'm about to have my hand raised in victory after one of the 13 pins I had as a rookie wrestler at Pillsbury Baptist Bible College in Owatonna, Minnesota, during the 1966-1967 wrestling year.*

AUTHOR BIOGRAPHY - Dr. Tom Latham

Dr. Latham's full name is Harry Thomas Latham, but to his friends, he is Tom. His Brazilian friends know him as Pastor Thomas. He publishes under his pen name, Dr. Tom Latham. His remarkable career as a missionary in Brazil spans more than 50 years. Many factors contributed to his success, but above all, his resolute faith in Jesus Christ, his personal Savior, had the greatest impact.

Tom became a Christian while serving in the U.S. Navy, where he began holding Protestant Divine Services whenever his ship was at sea. After completing his naval service, he spent the next four years at Bible college to further his spiritual journey. Graduation from Central Baptist Theological Seminary earned him a Master of Divinity (MDiv) degree. He achieved a significant milestone in his studies by earning a Doctor of Ministry (DMin) degree from Luther Rice Seminary.

Tom met Penny Stimpson, and together they began a mission to serve God in Brazil. Their family grew to include three children, six grandchildren, and eleven great-grandchildren. Together, they started four churches in Brazil.

Tom led extremely successful wrestling programs in many public schools for more than 20 years, including training and coaching. His church team won the Brazilian National Title in 2010 and the State Title in 2013.

Although Penny was promoted to glory (passed away), Tom continues to serve Christ in Brazil.

Read many details about Dr. Latham and his educational journey at www.brazilwrestler.com.

ACKNOWLEDGEMENTS

I acknowledge Jesus Christ, my Savior. Without His guidance and grace lifting me from a spiritual ditch, this book would not exist. I owe Him more than I can ever repay.

I thank my three children, Thomas, Shane, and Kosette, for making life an adventure as we faced the challenges and joys of the mission field in Brazil. Their companionship gave us more experiences than I could capture in my more than 70 manuscripts, which may eventually become published books.

I also thank Dave Carlson, owner of DynoTech Publishing, a proper Jack of all trades and master of MANY, for his invaluable contribution to the editing and publishing process. His tremendous efforts far exceeded what I could have accomplished alone, and I am deeply grateful. His excellent command of the English language helped bring my words to life. Dave, a brother wrestler who resides in Colorado Springs, Colorado, stays busy during retirement with consulting projects related to computer technology, computer-aided illustration, book editing, and publishing.

Books by Dr. Tom Latham

www.brazilwrestler.com/book/

AUTOBIOGRAPHY

Exceptional opportunity to examine a 50-year professional journey, brought to life through 130+ vibrant color images.

Into the Light: Half-Century as Missionaries in Brazil (ISBN 978-1-885708-19-9)

Other Books

Brazilian Adventures (ISBN 978-1-885708-25-0)
Why Missionaries Quit (ISBN 978-1-885708-27-4)

SHANE WOODS SERIES

www.shanewoods.com

1: *The Snow Peak Robbers* (ISBN 978-1-885708-51-9)
2: *The Strawberry Fair* (ISBN 978-1-885708-52-6)
3: *The Buzzard Butte Poachers* (ISBN978-1-885708-53-3)
4: *The Eastern Rodeo* (ISBN 978-1-885708-54-0)
5: *The Linn County Vandals* (ISBN 978-1-885708-55-7)
6: *The Nez Perce Treasure* (ISBN 978-1-885708-56-6)
7: *The Mountain Lion* (ISBN 978-1-885708-57-1)
8: *The Precarious Plane Ride* (ISBN 978-1-885708-58-8)
9: *The Empty Coffin Mystery* (ISBN 978-1-885708-59-5)

Planned for 2026:
10: *The State Championship* (ISBN 978-1-885708-60-1)
11: *The Baseball Problem* (ISBN 978-1-885708-61-8)

www.ingramcontent.com/pod-product-compliance
Lightning Source LLC
Chambersburg PA
CBHW050029040726
47599CB00015B/1607

* 9 7 8 1 8 8 5 7 0 8 5 9 5 *